"We'll have to do t[...]
I've enjoyed it."

"Me too."

He smiled and scratched his head. "Like I said, I've never bared my soul like this to someone your age. You're very much like your grandmother. Not just your physical features, but your personality as well. You have her generous, caring heart, and her decency and integrity."

"There's a reason for that, Rand." *If I don't tell him the truth now, I might never find the courage!*

He grinned. "Good genes, I suppose. And good upbringing."

"There's more." She was trembling now. "It's a long story."

He took her elbow and urged her toward the door. "Can we save it for our next date? I really need to see my grandmother before she thinks I've dropped off the face of the earth."

Her resolve crumbled. "I suppose so."

As he drove her home, Becky's heart did emotional flip-flops. The door was opening for a relationship with Rand Cameron, but would her deception destroy their love before it even had a chance to blossom?

Residing in Southern California with Bill, her husband of 37 years, **CAROLE GIFT PAGE**, award-winning author of 44 books, once had a job sculpting heads out of clay for a man who makes ventriloquist dummies. Today, Carole teaches and speaks at churches and conferences across the country on the topic of "Becoming a Woman of Passion." She and her sister Susan, a talented singer and ventriloquist, have formed a "Sister Act" and perform often for women's programs and retreats. Susan is accompanied by "Sam," whose head Carole sculpted. Carole also draws from her book, Misty, about the death of her fourth child—a newborn baby, to share how God can bring us amazing joy in the midst of our deepest sorrows. Carole taught creative writing at Biola University, La Mirada, California, and is on the Advisory Board of the American Christian Writers. She received the C.S. Lewis Honor Book Award and was a finalist several times for the prestigious Gold Medallion and Campus Life Book-of-the-Year Award. Besides Misty, Carole and Bill have three other children—Kimberle, David and Heather—and four darling grandchildren.

Beguiling Masquerade

Carole Gift Page

Heartsong Presents

*To my beautiful niece, Denise Geston, who loves to write
and whose sweet spirit blesses everyone she knows.*

A note from the Author:
*I love to hear from my readers! You may correspond with me
by writing:*

> **Carole Gift Page**
> **Author Relations**
> **PO Box 719**
> **Uhrichsville, OH 44683**

ISBN 1-59310-076-0

BEGUILING MASQUERADE

*Our mission is to publish and distribute inspirational products offering
exceptional value and biblical encouragement to the masses.*

All Scripture quotations are taken from the King James Version of the
Bible.

All of the characters and events in this book are fictitious. Any resem-
blance to actual persons, living or dead, or to actual events is purely
coincidental.

PRINTED IN THE U.S.

one

Professor Rand Cameron was waxing eloquent in his masterful baritone, the way he always did on Tuesdays and Thursdays in Sociology 304, and Becky Chandler couldn't take her eyes off him.

"Today's baby boomers are just beginning to experience the scourge of ageism," he trumpeted, straightening his muscular, six-foot frame for emphasis. "Think of it, people. The radical, freewheeling sixties generation that refused to trust anyone over thirty is on the brink of turning sixty!" His mouth did that quirky little turned-up-at-the-corner thing it always did when he was indulging in irony.

Becky's insides turned to mush. Oh no, she was pulling that routine again, swooning over her professor like a lovesick teenager. *This has got to stop, Rebecca. You're a mature, twenty-five-year-old woman, a graduate sociology major studying for her doctorate. You do not have a crush on your teacher!*

He leaned into the podium with a confident air, his tweed jacket endearingly rumpled, his tie askew. "And we can expect that today's intrepid senior citizens will summon the same moxie they showed decades ago to confront—and conquer—the challenges of aging."

But it's not that simple! They still face an uphill battle all the way! Becky raised her hand, waved it momentarily, then withdrew it.

Professor Cameron's dusky, blue-eyed gaze met hers. "Did you have a comment, Miss Chandler?"

The roof of her mouth suddenly felt as dry as sandpaper. She shook her head, her pulse skyrocketing. "No, uh, yes. I mean, no, Sir, Professor Cameron."

A quizzical smile played on his lips. "Hasn't this happened before, Miss Chandler? I sense you have something important to say, and yet the cat has got your tongue once again."

"It was nothing. A passing thought. . .I'm sorry, it's gone."

"Very well, Miss Chandler." He expelled a disgruntled sigh as his gaze swept over the rest of the class. "Then, as I was saying. . ."

Becky's face flamed. She reached back self-consciously, her fingers entwining a curl at the nape of her neck. She had done it again—turned into a bumbling idiot before the gorgeous, imposing Rand Cameron! Why could she never put together two coherent sentences in his presence?

After class, with pounding heart and sweaty palms, she approached him. She had to explain herself—make things right. He was standing at his desk riffling through papers. She cleared her throat. He towered over her, bigger than life, his azure eyes crinkling behind wire-rim spectacles. A lock of raven hair hung over his ruddy forehead, giving his handsome face an air of playfulness.

He surprised her with a wink. Not quite a wink, but close. "Yes, Miss Chandler? You finally have something to say?"

Heat crept up her face. She imagined her fair skin glowing crimson. "Yes. Terrific class, Professor Cameron." No other words came. Clutching her books to her chest, she turned on her heel and fled the classroom before her dignity was shredded.

Hours later, still smarting over her humiliation, Becky arrived at the Bermuda Bistro, her favorite off-campus eatery, just a stone's throw from the Pacific Ocean. Already she felt better. An hour of conversation with her friend, Lyn Orcutt, would brighten her spirits. Lyn, a postgraduate theater arts major, was already there for their usual Tuesday night outing. Dinner at the Bistro gave them a few carefree hours of escape from the heavy academic milieu of Rockmount College.

They were seated at a small table on a rustic patio framed by white trellises with climbing ivy. After ordering iced tea and seafood salads they turned toward the waning sunlight painting the city skyline with burnished hues.

"Hey, Girlfriend, look at that view! It's a perfect California evening." Lyn pushed back a thatch of fiery red hair from her round face and smiled. "If only we had a couple of handsome men to enjoy the sunset with us."

Becky poked at her salad. "Speak for yourself. The only man I care about thinks I'm a babbling fool."

"The good professor?"

"Who else?"

"What now?"

"Don't ask!" Becky set her fork on the checkered tablecloth and leaned forward. "Look at me, Lyn. What do you see?"

Lyn nibbled a shrimp, her stubby pinky arched just so. "I see an attractive girl in a jersey shirt and denim jumper with a figure to die for. I'd die for it. I see someone who's smart and funny and kind. . .my best friend since grade school."

"No, that's not what I mean. What's wrong with me?"

"Nothing! You're just a little. . .verbally challenged around certain people."

"But why? I'm an articulate person. I can talk. I'm not afraid of people. I lead a Bible study for high school kids without missing a beat. And you know how ruthless teenagers can be. But they don't scare me. Nobody scares me, except—"

"The good professor."

Becky nodded. "I know it's crazy, Lyn, but he's everything I've ever dreamed of in a man. He's clever and intelligent, a lawyer who cares more about the rights of the downtrodden than he does about making money. And he's a wonderful teacher, yet he doesn't come across as stuffy or bookish. He's got this sense of humor that's so subtle, half the class doesn't get it. But I do. And did I tell you he teaches a Sunday school class of sixth grade boys?"

"You've told me. Once or twice. . .maybe a dozen times."

"Well, what guy is brave enough to do that?"

"I know, Beck. And I've seen that big, thumb-worn Bible on his desk. He's every Christian girl's Mr. Right. And he's also taken."

Becky bristled. "Not exactly."

"Then who is that willowy blond I see hanging on his arm every chance she gets?"

Becky forked up a wedge of avocado. "Gloria Farrington is not the one for Rand Cameron."

"Oh, really? And who appointed you his romance guardian?"

"Whoa, whose side are you on, Lyn?"

"My best friend's. And when I see her walking open-eyed into a minefield, I've got to warn her. The talk on campus is that the two of them will be engaged before the semester's over."

"If he marries her, he'll be the one walking through a minefield. They have nothing in common. He's into ministry and serving humanity and all that good stuff. She's out for number one. She has a heart of stone and claws like fish-hooks, and we both know the fish she's trying to land."

Lyn made a sad little face. "And if you ask me, Girlfriend, she's already got him, hook, line, and sinker."

Becky's fervor drained away. "Meanwhile, I'm practically incoherent in his presence."

Lyn stirred a spoonful of sugar into her iced tea. "Being tongue-tied does limit the potential for a romantic future."

"Don't you think I know it? If only we could break the ice and carry on an ordinary conversation!"

"When is the last time you tried?"

"Today. I tried to comment on his lecture, but as usual I clammed up."

"Bummer."

"I also wanted his advice about my dissertation. My topic is due next week, and I still can't decide what to write on."

"I thought you were writing about old people."

"Of course. I am specializing in gerontology."

"I know the drill. You're going to be a geriatric therapist and all that. So what's the problem?"

"I can't decide what my thesis statement should be."

"Simple. We all get old. The elderly are the only minority we all end up becoming. So be good to them. You will be one soon."

Becky choked back a chuckle. "You said it better than I could."

"Okay, next problem."

"I'm writing about the ways people discriminate against the elderly. I've done a ton of research and dozens of interviews with senior citizens. But I need something more. A hook. Something that goes beyond textbook theories and statistics."

"Like what?"

Becky nudged a cherry tomato around her salad bowl. "I don't know, Lyn. I feel like I'm on the outside looking in. It's like Scripture says about seeing through a glass darkly. I'm not getting the real picture."

"That's easy, Girlfriend. You need to take your thesis outside the cloistered world of academia and test it in the rushing waters of real life."

Becky laughed. Lyn had a way of making everything dramatic. "I suppose you're right. I wish I could get inside the skin of an old person for a day and see how the world treats me."

"Then do it."

"Do what?"

"Get inside the skin of an old person."

"That was just a figure of speech."

"But I'm serious, Becky. Put on a disguise. Become an old

lady for a day. Walk the streets and see how people treat you. I predict it will be quite a shock to you."

An undercurrent of excitement prickled Becky's skin. "You mean, actually dress up, with a wig and makeup and frumpy clothes?"

"Sure. Remember when I played that old woman in our theater production of *Arsenic and Old Lace* last year?"

"The Brewster sisters! Two old spinsters poisoning old men who come to their home. How could I forget?"

"I played Abby Brewster. You couldn't believe it was me, remember?"

"As I recall, you took a class in theatrical makeup and did your own. It was fantastic."

"I could whip up a disguise for you that would fool your own mother."

"It's funny you should suggest that. I remember studying about a woman who did that very thing."

"Dressed up like an old lady?"

"It must have been twenty years ago or more. She disguised herself as an octogenarian. Her name was Pat. Pat Moore. If I remember right, she stayed in character on and off for several years. She was even beaten by a gang of thugs. It was an amazing story."

"What happened to her?"

"She became an industrial designer. She's done all sorts of innovative things to help the elderly."

"Well then, see, Beck? You'll be following in the tradition of a brave and exemplary researcher."

Becky's pulse quickened. "I'd have to get my faculty advisor's approval."

"Naturally. Meanwhile, I'll work on some ideas and scrounge up some thrift shop clothes. Tell you what. Meet me backstage at the campus theater next Saturday. When I'm finished with you, you won't believe your eyes."

❧

One thing Becky could say about Lyn Orcutt: She was a woman of her word. Becky knew she was in for a remarkable experience as soon as she surveyed the paraphernalia Lyn had gathered—a silver-gray wig, latex mask, spectacles, a lumpy bodysuit complete with dowager's hump, orthopedic shoes, support stockings, a dowdy skirt and sweater, a worn pillbox hat with a veil, a walking cane, and white gloves.

Becky shook her head. "It's a cinch no one will recognize me in this getup."

"That's the idea. The only way your research will be authentic is if no one knows you're in disguise, except for me and your advisor, of course."

"That means I keep Professor Cameron out of the loop?"

"Absolutely."

Becky tried on the latex mask and wig and stared at herself in the mirror. "Look at me, Lyn. I can't believe I'm doing this."

Lyn adjusted Becky's mask, smoothing it gently around the eyes and mouth. "This could work, Beck, but what would be better is a customized prosthetic mask."

"What's that?"

"I'll need to make a plaster cast of your face, then mold latex pieces contoured to fit your features."

"A plaster cast? You mean, like a death mask?"

"I know it sounds awful, but it'll be worth it."

"Are you saying I'll have to lie still while you slather wet plaster all over my face?"

Lyn grinned. "What are best friends for?"

"Sounds to me like a case of claustrophobia waiting to happen."

"It's no worse than a medieval torture chamber." Lyn sashayed over to a workbench and began rummaging through canisters and boxes. "I'm kidding. It's not that bad. How do you think I got my mask for *Arsenic and Old Lace?*"

Becky took a backward step, warning signals dancing in her brain. "H—how will I breathe?"

"Simple. A couple of drinking straws in your nostrils. And a good coating of petroleum jelly goes on your lashes and brows. When the plaster hardens I'll pry it off your face and we'll be ready to transform you into an octogenarian. So how about it? Are you ready?"

"Ready or not, let's do it." Becky gazed at herself in the mirror. Even in Lyn's ill-fitting mask and wig, she felt like someone else, a person she didn't quite know. What would it be like when the disguise was complete and she ventured out into a callous, unsuspecting world? *What am I getting myself into? Where will this bizarre journey take me? And will I ever be the same again?*

two

It took only a few days for Becky Chandler to age over fifty years. She couldn't believe the transformation. Staring back at her in the floor-length mirror in her small apartment was a stooped, wrinkled, antiquated woman who looked faintly familiar. Of course! Her grandmother, the woman she had been named after. Rebecca Sterling had been dead for years now, but Becky would never forget her—a genteel lady of great character, strength, and faith.

Lyn broke into her thoughts, reminding Becky of her presence. "So what do you think? Isn't it amazing?"

"I can't believe it's me." Becky moved her fingertips over the lifelike latex wrinkles creasing her neck and chin. "Will it stay in place? I don't want to be out someplace and have my face start peeling off."

"Don't worry. The spirit gum will hold everything in place. Just be careful when you eat. Your lips aren't covered. Too much liquid could loosen the latex around them."

Becky tried to smile, but her face felt stiff, uncomfortable, unyielding. "I don't know if I'll ever get used to this contraption on my face, not to mention this lumpy bodysuit." She turned sideways and studied her sagging silhouette.

Lyn nudged her. "Guess what! I'm not jealous of your figure anymore."

Becky elbowed her back. "You're enjoying this entirely too much!"

"What's not to love? I got to change my best friend from a shapely, radiant brunette into a drab, doddering crone!"

"Thanks. I'll remember you in my will."

"Actually, you don't look half bad for an eighty year old."

13

"Come on, I don't look a day over seventy-five!"

"And weren't the pale blue contact lenses a stroke of genius? They make your eyes look weathered and faded."

"And the elastic bandages give me ankles an elephant would envy." Becky struck an exaggerated pose, folding her arms over her baggy brown sweater. "But at least now I won't have to send out questionnaires to nursing homes and retirement communities. I'll find out firsthand what it's like to be old."

Lyn squeezed her arm. "But you're not ready yet. You may look like an elderly woman. But now you've got to get the voice and the body language right."

"Great. My goose is cooked. I could never be the actress you are."

"Don't worry, I'll give you a crash course. The voice first. Try lowering your voice a notch and speak just above a whisper."

"Is this what you have in mind?" Becky rasped.

"That's good. Just a touch lower and a bit louder."

"How's this?"

"Good. That's it."

"It's killing my throat."

"All the better. The raspiness will come naturally. Now for your body language. Walk a little."

Becky crossed the room in her usual smooth stride. "This won't do, will it?"

"You look too healthy, too full of energy, and too mobile. You need to move as if every joint and muscle were aching. Try again. Not so fluid. That's it. Slow, careful, deliberate gestures."

Becky moved with a halting gait. "I think I'm getting it."

"Bend your back a little. Good. Now crane your neck a bit. And keep your arms close to your sides. That's it, your steps shorter, a little uncertain."

"I want to look elderly, not disabled."

Lyn handed her the cane. "Use this. Remember, your

vision is probably clouded with cataracts. And your hearing isn't what it used to be."

Becky shuffled back across the room and studied herself in the mirror. "It's uncanny. I feel as if I'm looking at a stranger."

Lyn nodded. "You're going to pull this off, Girlfriend. No one would guess it was you."

Remembering to keep her body stiff, Becky lowered herself onto the sofa. She started to cross her legs, then caught herself. "There's still more I have to do, Lyn."

"What's that?"

"I can't go out and face the world until I know who I am. I've got to have a history. A dossier of this woman's life. She's got to be a real person to me. She's got to be me. I've got to know what a woman born in the 1920s feels like. . .what it felt like being a teenager during the Second World War, a young bride in the 1950s, a mother in the sixties, a grandmother in the eighties."

"Beck, don't make this more complicated than it is."

"But what do I say when people ask me about myself?"

"Say as little as possible and stay as close to the truth as you can."

"What truth?" Becky pulled at a fray on her sweater. "This whole thing is a deception. That's the only thing that bothers me about going out in disguise. I'm deceiving people without even saying a word."

Lyn sat down beside her. "You're doing research for a very good cause, Beck. It's a legitimate method for gathering information."

"I know. They even have a name for it. The participant-observer."

"Well, see? You want to help people understand what it's like to be old so the next time they encounter an elderly person, they won't be cruel or thoughtless. They won't discriminate against people just because they're old."

Becky clapped her gloved hands. "I've got it. I'll be my grandmother. I'll use her history. When I'm in these clothes and makeup, I'm Rebecca Sterling."

"Sounds like a plan!" Lyn stood up and held out her hand. "So what do you say, Rebecca Sterling? Are you ready to face your public?"

"Almost. Just one more thing." Becky motioned Lyn back down beside her. "Pray with me first. This is going to be uncharted territory. I don't know what to expect. Or what hot water I might get myself into. All I know is, I don't want to do anything that's not glorifying to God."

After praying together for several minutes, they left Becky's apartment and walked down a flight of stairs to Lyn's late model sedan in the parking lot. "I'm driving you," Lyn announced.

"You don't have to. I can take my own car."

"No way. Get in. I'm not going to have it on my conscience if you get mugged on your first day as an old lady."

Becky knew better than to argue with her best friend. With a hapless shrug, she climbed into the passenger seat and fastened her seat belt over her well-padded middle.

It was only a ten-minute drive to Las Rosas, a thriving town a dozen miles south of San Francisco and just a hop, skip, and a jump from lovely Half Moon Bay. But the drive seemed to take forever. Glancing over at Lyn, Becky was painfully aware of the disparity between the two of them. Lyn was an attractive, robust young woman with flame-red hair; Becky was now a bent, wrinkled old lady with a nest of gray hair and ragamuffin clothes. Her vanity rose in silent protest. *Please, God, if I run into any of the guys from campus, don't let them know it's me!*

In the heart of downtown Las Rosas, Lyn parked at the curb near an upscale department store. "Listen, Beck, this is your first time out like this, so I'm not letting you out of my sight. While you walk up the block and back, I'll be watching from the car. If you need me, just wave your cane."

"It's no big deal, Lyn. I'll be fine." She slipped out of the car and stepped gingerly onto the sidewalk. Glancing around through her clear glass spectacles, she adjusted her pillbox hat and straightened the folds of her long skirt. *Help me, heavenly Father. Let me learn from this experience what You want me to learn. Help me to honor You. Lead me where You want me to go. Calm my nervous heart and give me Your courage.*

Becky—Rebecca—shuffled down the block away from Lyn's car. She held her thrift shop handbag close and leaned on her cane with every step. She gazed into storefront windows as if interested in the merchandise. The pencil-thin mannequins sported only youthful garments; there was nothing on display for an eighty-year-old woman.

She shambled on, eyeing passersby with a covert glance. No one noticed her; nobody looked her way. She could be invisible. It was an odd sensation. She was used to walking down the street or entering a room and having people glance her way, offer an approving smile, acknowledge her presence somehow, with a nod or a word or at least a hint of curiosity. Men often gazed at her with a look that made her blush or turn her face away. She had always dressed modestly to minimize such stares. But there was no chance of such ogling today!

At the corner she waited for the electric signal. When it flashed green, she scuffled across the street in the slow, loping gait she had practiced. She was only halfway across when the light turned red. A vehicle came careening around the corner toward her, the driver's hand hard on the horn. She leapt to the curb, forgetting her antiquated persona. She gripped her cane and inhaled deeply. *What if I hadn't been able to move so fast? I'd be a grease spot on the pavement!*

She ambled on, her heart hammering. *Make a mental note.*

Be extra careful crossing the street! In fact, maybe this old lady should invest in a skateboard!

Already she had decided it wasn't fun being old. *So this is what I have to look forward to. Is this why You let us grow old and frail, Lord—so we'll appreciate heaven more?* Her latex mask felt itchy and her padded bodysuit and heavy garments were warm and confining under the glare of the September California sun. Her throat was dry too. She should have brought her bottled water, but there was no room for it in her small pocketbook.

A drugstore was just ahead. She'd stop and buy a cola. Old people drank cola, didn't they? Just as she started to push the heavy door open, two young men in leather jackets came bounding out. The force of the swinging door nearly toppled her. She fell back against the stucco wall and caught her balance as the youths swept past her. One—a barrel-chested fellow with rings in his ears and nose—looked back and snarled, "Watch where you're going, you old hag!"

For an instant shame washed over her, and she had the fleeting impulse to apologize. Just as quickly reason returned, followed by white-hot anger. She lifted her skirts, raised her cane in the air, and galumphed after the two men. In her natural voice she shouted, "Next time watch how you treat old ladies!"

The two men stopped, stared back dumbfounded, then shrugged and swaggered on down the street.

Rebecca slunk back to the drugstore and went inside, making sure the way was clear. At the counter she adjusted her sagging pillbox hat and patted her windblown gray hair into place. After all the excitement, a cold drink would taste good. A young woman stood behind the counter thumbing through a magazine. *Surely she'll notice me in a minute.* Rebecca cleared her throat. The woman glanced up, then looked back at her magazine. Rebecca fished in her purse for a dollar. In her raspy voice, she said, "I'd like a cola please."

The woman kept reading.

Maybe she didn't hear me. Rebecca moved on down the counter toward the woman and repeated her request.

With a perturbed sigh, the woman set down her magazine, reached for the bottle, and thumped it down hard on the counter. "What's your hurry, Lady? You got someplace important to go?"

Rebecca handed her the money. "As a matter of fact, I do." *Oh no, my real voice again!*

"How did you do that?" quizzed the girl. "You sounded like a normal person."

Rebecca gritted her teeth. "I am a normal person."

"I mean, you don't sound old."

"I'm getting older by the minute!" Rebecca pivoted and strode toward the door, then realized she had left her cane leaning against the counter. She turned around, stalked back, and retrieved the cane with an exaggerated flourish while the young woman gaped at her.

Becky had had enough of being old for one day. She made her way back to Lyn's car, climbed inside, laid her head back, and closed her eyes. "Oh, Lyn, I never want to be old."

"That bad?"

"Worse!"

"What happened?"

Becky met Lyn's gaze. "Other than being ignored and insulted, nearly getting run over by an impatient driver, hit by a swinging door, and trampled by two idiots, I'm perfectly fine." She yanked off her hat and wig and shook her hair free. "No, I'm not fine. My head hurts from this hideous wig, my eyes sting from the contact lenses, this sweater is hot and scratchy, the elastic bandages are too tight on my ankles, my face itches, and I feel like a mummy in King Tut's tomb!"

Lyn drummed her fingers on the steering wheel. "Other than that, don't you think your first time went quite well?"

They both broke into laughter.

Becky clasped her latex face. "Don't make me laugh. My cheeks will crack!"

Lyn struggled to stifle herself. "At least you came back alive."

"Just barely. I can't believe it, Lyn. I'm more feisty as an old lady than I am as me. I was ready to tackle those two guys who shoved me and called me an old hag." Becky pulled off her white gloves, finger by finger. "To tell the truth, what hurt most was being called an old hag."

Lyn shrugged. "I've been called worse. Sorry, Beck, I should have warned you. I experienced some of the same things in costume as Abby Brewster, but not all in one afternoon!"

"Well, I shouldn't have lost my cool the way I did. How am I ever going to do my research if I let myself lose control?"

"Most people have a lifetime to get used to being old. You've only had a couple of days."

Becky nodded. "It's culture shock for me, that's for sure. But now I'd better go home and write everything down in my journal, even the way I messed up."

Lyn turned the ignition. "It'll be better next time."

"Will it? I'm not even sure where to go or what to do."

"Maybe you should pick a more controlled and predictable environment."

"Like what?"

Lyn pulled away from the curb and accelerated. "Like a nursing home or retirement center. Someplace where you can get to know senior citizens on equal terms. As a peer. As someone they can trust as a friend."

Becky gazed out the window. "What if they see through me? Do you really think I can pull it off?"

"There's only one way to find out. Why don't you go visit the Morning Glory Nursing Home? It's close to the campus and your apartment. You could even walk over and back whenever you pleased."

"True. I bet I could slip in and out without being noticed. It's perfect! You've just made my day, Lyn."

On Saturday morning, with Lyn's help, Becky donned her Rebecca Sterling disguise and walked the five blocks from her apartment to the Morning Glory Nursing Home. The facility was a long, one-story stucco building bearing the lackluster architectural style of the late sixties. Its Spartan decor was punctuated by thriving greenery—a startling blend of bougainvillea and tropical, bright-orange birds of paradise. The entrance was noteworthy if only for its wide porch and pillars, which lent a mismatched colonial aura to the unadorned building.

But it wasn't the garish architecture that troubled Rebecca. It was the prospect of facing people who would surely see through her disguise and feel she was perpetrating a terrible offense. They would think she was deceiving them, mocking, even ridiculing them. They would have nothing but contempt for her. And how could she blame them?

Leaning heavily on her cane, Rebecca maneuvered her sagging body up the porch steps. As her gloved fingers turned the doorknob, she felt her stomach knot. *I don't even know what I'm going to say or do. I should have developed a plan. Dear Lord, help me not to make a complete fool of myself. Lead me to the people You want me to talk with. Teach me Your truths, Father. And let me minister in some way to these dear folks.*

She shuffled across the tiled lobby to the information desk, her cane clicking rhythmically on the floor. Behind the wide, utilitarian desk sat a square-jawed woman talking on the phone. She could have been forty, or sixty. *Funny how I never paid attention to age, until now.* The swarthy woman held up one sturdy finger and continued talking. With her white uniform, she could have been a nurse. Or maybe not. Her coarse, gray-black hair was pulled back in a bun, but she wore no nurse's cap. Her badge read "Amarilla."

Rebecca gazed around the room at the small groupings of sofas and chairs occupied by people watching television or simply sitting, staring into space. A few sat in wheelchairs; others moved about with walkers. Four people sat at a small table playing cards.

But this was certainly no vacation resort. Even with its bright artificial flowers and prosaic watercolor prints, this place had the dreary ambiance of a convalescent hospital. Most unmistakable was the ubiquitous smell of disinfectant and urine that seemed the bane of nursing homes.

On one wall near the desk was a bulletin board covered with photographs with a neatly printed name beneath each one. *These are the people who live here. Do they realize what a dead end this is? Are they miserable or content? Or just resigned? Is this what we all face if death doesn't claim us first?*

She swallowed over a lump in her throat. This was going to be harder than she expected. How could she intrude on these people's lives just for the sake of her research project? It suddenly seemed an incredibly selfish thing to do.

Becky, get yourself out of here before that lady gets off the phone. You were crazy to come here. You're asking for trouble if you stay!

Rebecca turned toward the door just as the woman behind the desk said, "May I help you?"

Rebecca hesitated, her thoughts whirling. *Speak in your raspy voice. You've come this far, you've got to carry on the charade. But what if she sees through me?* "I. . .I came to visit my friend." Where had that come from? What friend?

"What is your friend's name?"

In desperation Rebecca scanned the photos on the bulletin board. One bright, smiling face drew her. "Myrtle Watson," she heard herself say.

"And your name is. . . ?"

"Rebecca. Rebecca Sterling."

Amarilla's eyes narrowed.

Rebecca took an uncertain step backward. *Does she suspect me? Does she wonder why a college girl would traipse around in a getup like this?*

"Myrtle's room is on the right, just down the hall. Room 110. Usually only her grandson comes to visit."

"Oh, well, I. . .I just thought. . ."

Amarilla smiled for the first time, her dark eyes as bright as buttons. "It's good for Myrtle to have a friend visit her. She loves people. And they love her."

Rebecca nodded and averted her gaze before Amarilla read the truth in her eyes. *I've never met Myrtle Watson, and now I'm pretending to be her long-lost friend!*

three

The door to room 110 was ajar. Music filtered from the room, what sounded like contemporary Christian praise music. Rebecca stood at the door, her hand poised to knock. *Heavenly Father, let me be doing this for the right reasons. Help me to find the truth You have for me here. And let me be a blessing to this dear lady who has no idea who I am or why I've come.*

Rebecca drew in a deep breath and knocked. When there was no response, she knocked louder. Finally a soft, lilting voice called, "Come in."

Rebecca gripped her cane, gave the door a gentle push, and shuffled inside. Her eyes rested on a diminutive lady sitting in a hospital bed, a large Bible on her lap. She was wearing a pink cotton duster with ruffled sleeves that nearly covered her thin, gnarled hands. A wreath of gray-white hair framed a porcelain face lined with wrinkles the way an heirloom cup might be lined with fine cracks. Her eyes were a sapphire blue behind wire-rim spectacles and her weathered cheeks had a rosy blush that matched her pursed lips.

"Good morning," she crooned. "Are you looking for me?"

Rebecca approached the bed, mentally summoning her raspy voice. "I–I'm here to see Myrtle Watson."

"That's me. Come in." She nodded toward an overstuffed chair beside the bed. "Sit down and visit a spell."

Rebecca made her way to the chair and sat down with slow, deliberate movements. *Now what, Lord? What do I say to this woman?*

Smiling, Myrtle stretched out knobby fingers to Rebecca.

"I hope you'll forgive me, Dear. My memory isn't what it used to be. I can't recall your name."

"Rebecca. Rebecca Sterling."

They clasped hands.

"Of course, Dear. I remember. We were on the committee to raise money for the Crippled Children's Society years ago."

"Not exactly."

"Then it was the women's auxiliary at church!"

"No, not church either." Rebecca's face grew warm under her latex mask. She couldn't do this. It was cruel to deceive this elderly woman. She hoisted herself to her feet. "I really can't stay."

Myrtle's face darkened. "But you just got here."

"I know, but—"

Myrtle closed her Bible. "I'm sorry I didn't recognize you, Miss Sterling. It's these old eyes."

Rebecca placed her gloved hand over Myrtle's. "No, that's not it. You don't know me, and I shouldn't intrude on you."

"But, Dear, you're not intruding. I love company. Please, sit down. Stay awhile and talk to me."

With misgivings, Rebecca sat back down.

Myrtle's smile rivaled the sun shining through the chintz curtains. "You did say your name is Rebecca? You must be new at the home. Will you be living here?"

"No, I'm just visiting. The truth is, I saw your smiling face on the bulletin board, and I wanted to get acquainted. Do you mind?"

"Not at all, Dear. We old gals have to stick together. Friendships are important at our age."

Nodding, Rebecca stole a glance around the room. It was small and unadorned, with nondescript furniture—a highboy and dresser, two chairs, a nightstand, and a movable tray table. A walker stood by the bed. A vase of artificial flowers, a photo album, and a framed photograph of a young boy graced the highboy. A telephone and water pitcher sat on the nightstand. On the wall above the bed hung a framed print of a Monet landscape done in gentle pastels. A framed console near the ceiling on the opposite wall held a portable television set.

Myrtle fumbled in the folds of her blanket for the TV remote control unit and turned down the sound. "There. Now we can talk. Tell me the truth, Dear. Is your family planning to put you here in Morning Glory?"

The question was so startling and unexpected, Rebecca nearly blurted no in her natural voice. Recovering quickly, she rasped, "Most of my family is out of state." It was true. She was an only child, and her parents lived in Seattle. Aunts, uncles, and cousins were scattered throughout the Pacific Northwest.

"You have no one here in town, Dear? How do you manage?"

I manage just fine! I'm a twenty-five-year-old graduate student at Rockmount College! Rebecca twisted a tuft of fringe on her crocheted shawl. "I get along quite well in a small but comfortable apartment. Nothing fancy. And I do stay active."

"Oh, well, that's a relief. Living alone isn't easy. A body can't be too careful these days."

Somehow Rebecca had to get the spotlight off herself. "What about you, Myrtle? May I call you Myrtle?"

"My dear, of course you may. Everyone's called me Myrtle for eighty years."

"Do you have family here in town?"

Myrtle gazed over at the yellowed photograph on the bureau. "My grandson is all I have left. He's a wonderful lad. Visits nearly every day."

The photo showed a sober-faced boy in a sailor suit. The sadness in his eyes made her wince. "It must make you happy that he's so attentive."

A smile lingered on Myrtle's lips. "I raised him myself, you know."

"Did you really?"

"His parents—my daughter and son-in-law—died in a car crash when he was a boy. Eight years old. So young to know such sorrow."

"I'm sorry."

"My husband, Philip, and I took the lad in and loved him with all our hearts. He was quiet and sensitive, wise beyond his years. When he was fourteen, my husband died, leaving the boy and me to manage alone."

"That must have taken great courage."

Myrtle shrugged her frail shoulders. "With God's help, we made it through."

Rebecca shifted in her chair, her guilt and uneasiness growing. This poor woman was confiding too much. It was time to go. As she raised herself up, her cane clattered to the floor. She bent too quickly to retrieve it.

Myrtle noticed. "Be careful, Dear. You'll throw your back out and end up in here like me. You hold on to your independence as long as you can. It's one of the most precious gifts God gives us."

Rebecca heaved a sigh. *That was close! Thankfully, she isn't suspicious!*

Disappointment thickened Myrtle's voice. "Are you leaving already?"

Rebecca straightened her white gloves. "I really must go."

"You will come back, won't you?"

The question caught Rebecca by surprise. "You want me to?"

Myrtle folded her thin arms across her chest. "Indeed I do. This is a lonely place. I spend most of the day in this bed. My grandson comes to visit, of course, but he's young and doesn't say much. He doesn't know what it's like being old."

Rebecca brightened. "Yes, I'd love to come back and visit some more."

"Wonderful. But before you go, Dear. . ." Crooking her

finger, Myrtle beckoned Rebecca over and whispered confidentially, "I hope I'm not speaking out of turn, but I have some face cream you might like to try."

"Face cream?"

Myrtle pointed her arthritic index finger at Rebecca's latex-covered face. "You must have spent many years in the sun, Dear, to damage your skin like that. But this cream truly works wonders."

Rebecca stifled a chuckle. "Thank you, Myrtle. Next time I come I'll be sure to try it."

ે

Over the next two weeks Rebecca paid Myrtle Watson several visits and was amazed she could feel such camaraderie with a woman over three times her age. Each visit seemed to pass more quickly than the last. Sometimes they sat and chatted together, other times they watched reruns on television or played Chinese checkers. Several times they prayed together. Rebecca didn't want to admit that their visits meant more to her than they possibly could to the elderly woman. The friendship they were forming spanned the ages, went beyond time and years; it was a melding of kindred spirits, two souls connecting in spite of very different circumstances.

But is it honest? Am I being fair to Myrtle to let her invest her emotions in a friendship with someone who isn't what she seems to be? Or does age really matter? I love her as a friend regardless of my age. Oh, dear Lord, why does the right and wrong of this situation have to be so elusive?

Rebecca usually brought Myrtle some candy or fruit or a large-print book from the library. One day in mid-October she brought a small tape recorder and cassette tapes of her pastor's sermons. Myrtle nearly cried as she related that she hadn't been out to church since coming to Morning Glory a year ago. "Once my old legs gave out, my grandson couldn't take care of me anymore. He tried, but he had to work long hours and I couldn't stay alone. Now, the best he can do is wheel me down to the chapel service in the recreation room." She sighed and lifted her sagging chin. "But God is good. He's with me whether I'm in my bed or in church."

"That's so true." Rebecca placed a gloved hand on Myrtle's arm. "How do you do it?"

"Do what, Dear?"

"Stay so positive, so upbeat? So joyful?"

Myrtle's eyes glistened with sudden tears while her thin lips arced in a smile that brightened her entire face. "When I was a girl, I asked Jesus into my heart. At the time I knew that was the only way I was ever going to see those pearly gates. What I didn't fully grasp at the time was that the very Spirit of God was going to take up residence in my heart. When He left this old earth, Jesus promised to send us the Great Comforter, and He meant it. The Holy Spirit is there comforting me every minute of every day and every minute of every dark night. I just keep a running conversation going with Jesus all the time, and He's never let me down."

Rebecca was so moved she nearly forgot her raspy voice. "I wish my faith was as strong as yours."

"Your faith is strong, Dear. I've heard you pray."

"I like to think I have strong faith. It's not hard to trust God when things are going well." Rebecca was speaking from her heart now. "But I'm not sure I could be so trusting and joyful in painful circumstances."

Myrtle patted her hand. "Joy shines brightest in the dark, Dear. It's a strange paradox, isn't it? In the darkest night of the soul, joy can bubble up like a fountain of hope. All because of Jesus. He is our joy."

Rebecca gave Myrtle an impulsive hug. How could she thank this dear lady who had helped her grasp a profound truth that could shape her entire life? Myrtle Watson had discovered one of life's most elusive secrets—how to be genuinely happy in spite of difficult circumstances. The truth went beyond anything Rebecca could communicate in her doctoral dissertation. It was a truth she wanted to learn to live for herself.

Myrtle placed a quivering hand on Rebecca's cheek. "Dear, I gave you some of my face cream weeks ago. Have you been using it faithfully?"

Rebecca drew back, her hands flying to her latex cheeks. Had she unwittingly exposed her secret in that brief, spontaneous embrace? "I—I'm afraid I've been a bit negligent."

Myrtle wagged her crooked finger. "The minute you get back to your apartment, you use that cream. It'll soften that skin right up."

Rebecca sank back into her chair and sighed with relief, clutching her cane as if it were a lifesaver. She could hardly find her voice. "I'll do that, Myrtle. I promise."

From the doorway came a deep voice, oddly familiar. "Promise what?"

Rebecca swiveled in her chair and looked up in astonishment. Surely it wasn't possible! There in the doorway stood Professor Rand Cameron, dashingly handsome, bigger than life. He was wearing a topcoat over his navy suit and carrying a bouquet of pink roses.

Rebecca caught herself before blurting out his name.

The professor met Rebecca's gaze. "I'm sorry. I didn't mean to interrupt. I didn't realize Grams—my grandmother—had company."

Grandmother? Rebecca's throat tightened. She thought she might choke to death right there on the spot. She couldn't have spoken now if her life depended on it.

Fortunately Myrtle spoke up. "Rand, Dear, this is the friend I've told you so much about. Rebecca Sterling. Rebecca, I'd like you to meet my grandson, Rand Cameron."

Professor Cameron crossed the room and placed the bouquet in Myrtle's hands, kissed her cheek, then turned and extended his hand to Rebecca. "It's good to meet you at last, Miss Sterling. My grandmother has nothing but good things to say about you."

Rebecca allowed him to take her gloved hand in his, but still no words would come. She felt as if she were shrinking before his eyes, spinning out of control, dissolving in a vortex of shock and shame. *Does he recognize me? Does he suspect I'm not who his grandmother thinks I am? Will he hate me for deceiving her?*

Rebecca realized he was still holding her hand, waiting for her to respond. She summoned all her courage and croaked in her raspiest voice, "It's a pleasure to meet you, Mr. Cameron."

Rand grinned and sat down at the foot of his grandmother's bed. "I hope you two ladies don't mind a gentleman caller. I've spent an entire day with my students, listening to excuses why projects weren't done or explaining why grades weren't better. I could use a little mature, nonconfrontational conversation."

"Does that mean you don't enjoy teaching?" Rebecca ventured in her raspy voice.

"Not at all. I love teaching. It beats practicing law by a mile. I enjoy the give-and-take with my students. They're challenging and unpredictable. I think I learn more from them than they learn from me."

Rebecca stifled a smile. "I'm sure that's not the case, Mr. Cameron. Or is it Professor Cameron?"

"Yes, but call me Rand, please. Any friend of Grams' is a friend of mine."

"Then please call me Rebecca."

He nodded. "It's a beautiful name."

"Biblical, actually."

"Yes, it certainly is."

Rebecca felt the knot of tension in her shoulders relax. Her disguise was working. The professor didn't recognize her. So far so good! Now if she could just excuse herself and slip out, she would be home free. She would just have to be careful not to visit when the professor was around. She clasped her cane and started to hoist herself up.

The good professor was immediately at her side, his hand on her elbow to assist her. Flustered, Rebecca sank back into the chair. Rand's closeness sent her senses reeling. Her face grew warm under the latex mask. *What if I faint dead away right here?* She could imagine Rand gathering her up in his arms and patting her face to revive her, only to discover that her wrinkles were latex, her body was padded with cotton batting, and her gray hair was a wig.

Amid her anxiety and confusion, she heard Rand say, "I hope you're not leaving on my account, Rebecca."

Myrtle chimed in. "Of course she's not leaving. You two are just getting acquainted."

Rebecca closed her eyes. This wasn't going well. The longer she remained in Rand's presence, the more likely she was to make a mistake and reveal her identity. *Lord, please get me out of this. You know the last thing I intended to do was deceive good people. I just wanted to do my research and find ways to help the elderly. Now I'm caught in a deception that could hurt us all!*

"Rebecca, are you feeling okay?"

"Yes, I—I'm fine, Professor Cameron."

"Rand, remember?"

"Rand it is."

"You do look a bit distracted. Are you sure you're okay?"

"I'm fair to middlin'." Where did that phrase come from? Grandmother Sterling, of course!

Myrtle was eyeing her closely now. "You do look a bit peaked, Dear."

Rebecca recalled another of her grandmother's expressions—plumb poorly. The description fit. Her skin was sweating and itching under the unrelenting latex. She could envision the professor staring wide-eyed at her as her face began to peel. There was a movie like that, wasn't there, where people's faces peeled back and revealed disgusting things? They were robots or little green men from Mars or some such thing. She clasped her cane with firm resolve. "I really must go home."

Rand was right there ready to help her up. "Do you have your car?"

Her mind raced. She could say yes, but it would be a lie. "No, I walked."

Rand looked puzzled. "You walked? All the way from your home?"

"It's not that far."

"But it's dark now. You can't be out walking alone,"

"I'll call a taxi."

"You'll do no such thing," said Myrtle. "My grandson will drive you."

Rebecca's adrenaline shot to the ceiling. "That's not necessary. I'm perfectly capable of getting myself home."

"It's not open to debate. I'll drive you." Rand helped her out of the chair and adjusted her shawl around her shoulders. They both bid Myrtle good night, then Rand took Rebecca's arm and walked her out to his luxury car. He opened the passenger door and with exquisite patience helped her ease her hunched body onto the seat, then handed her the cane.

As he pulled away from the curb, Rebecca sat numb with disbelief. Here she was at last with the man she adored, and he was convinced she was an old lady! What bitter irony!

From the corner of her eye she studied Rand's handsome profile. His lime aftershave mingled with the faint aroma of coffee and the rich smell of leather seats. His closeness and the warmth of the car gave her a heady, surreal feeling. She couldn't quite catch her breath. *This can't be real! This is a dream, a glorious, impossible dream. . .or maybe it's a nightmare!*

"Where do you live, Rebecca?"

She gave him the address. He would never know it was the home of his student, Rebecca Chandler.

"You were going to walk all this way?"

"Walking helps me stay in shape." Had she really said that? How stupid could she be? She was shaped like a bag of potatoes!

Rand was kind enough not to state the obvious. "I'm sure if more of us walked, we'd make it to a ripe old age too."

"Walking keeps me self-reliant." What did that mean? Usually she was speechless in Rand's presence. Now she couldn't keep quiet.

"Here we are." He pulled into her driveway, turned off the engine, and looked over at her. "That wasn't so bad. A long walk, but a short drive."

She reached for the door handle. "Thank you, Professor. . . uh, I mean, Rand."

"I'll get the door for you. But first. . ."

Her fingers tightened around her cane. *Here it comes! He's going to tell me he knows who I am, yank off my wig, and have a good laugh at my expense!*

"I just want you to know how much I appreciate the friendship you have with my grandmother."

Rebecca exhaled. "Please don't make a fuss over it."

"I can't help myself, Rebecca. It means the world to me. I love my grandmother very much. I'm sure she's told you our story."

Rebecca nodded. "I know she raised you. . . ."

"From the time I was eight, she was the only mother I knew. I could have grown up a miserable person, losing both my parents the way I did."

"I can't imagine how painful that must have been."

"With God's help and my grandmother's love, I got through

it. I grew up to be a normal person." He chuckled. "Of course, don't ask my students about that. They consider me a bit eccentric."

"No, they don't."

Rand gave her a quizzical glance. "You say that with such certainty."

She groped for words. "I mean, I don't know how they could; you seem very normal to me."

He laughed. "I'll take that as a compliment."

"Please do."

Rand shifted his torso and looked her in the eye. His thick ebony hair curled over his forehead and several strands inched onto his coat collar. Even in the darkness his blue eyes glistened like moonlight on water. He fished in his breast pocket and handed her a business card.

"What's this?"

"Whenever you want to visit my grandmother, give me a call, and if I'm free I'll drive you over. Her health and her spirits have been a hundred times better since you started visiting her."

"I'm sure you're exaggerating."

"I'm serious, Rebecca. My grandmother has always been a social butterfly. You know the type. They thrive on having other people around. She's not like me. I'm an introvert at heart."

"An introvert? You? But you're around people all the time."

"Yes, but I need to get alone to recharge my batteries. That's a sure sign of an introvert."

Rebecca nodded. "I'm one too."

"Are you? Yes, I can see it. You love people, but you can't be with them all the time."

"Exactly."

"It's not that we don't enjoy helping people, but if we're going to do our best, we have to get alone sometimes."

"I've always felt guilty for feeling that way," she admitted.

"You shouldn't. It's simply what you need to restore yourself. I think Jesus Himself was an introvert. He loved being with the people and helping them, but at times He had to get off by Himself."

"I never thought of it that way, the possibility of Jesus being an introvert."

"It's just a little theory of mine. But one thing I do know, He needed to spend hours, even days, alone with His heavenly Father."

"We all need that."

"It makes you think, doesn't it? If Jesus Himself needed to spend time alone with the Father, how much more do we need that?"

"That's one of my biggest challenges, carving out time alone with God."

Rand's voice softened. "I bet you have a lot of wisdom to share from all your years of living."

"I don't know about that. The more I learn, the more I realize I have to learn."

"And that's the beginning of wisdom." Rand opened his door. "I didn't mean to talk your ear off. I'd better get you inside before you get chilled."

She raised her gloved hand in alarm. "You don't need to walk me to my door. I can manage."

Ignoring her protests, he came around to her side of the car, helped her out, and escorted her up the porch steps, his hand firmly on her arm. He waited while she searched her handbag for her key. When she fumbled with the lock, he gallantly took the key and opened the door for her. "Good night, Rebecca. We'll do this again soon."

Not if I can help it! She managed a whispered good night, but her voice was nearly gone from talking so much in her raspy voice. Strange. She rarely talked this much as Becky Chandler.

Only after she had stepped inside and closed the door did

she hear Rand's footsteps as he returned to his car. She waited until his car pulled away, then yanked off her pillbox hat and wig. She leaned back against the door and heaved a sigh. Never would she have anticipated a night like this— part agony, part ecstasy. How did she get herself into a predicament like this?

I've just had my first "date" with the man of my dreams, and as far as he knows, I'm my own grandma!

four

The next few days were an emotional roller-coaster ride for Becky. She was gathering crucial material she needed for her dissertation, but at what cost? The serious ramifications of her masquerade were becoming increasingly apparent. She was developing two relationships that were of great significance to the young Becky, but the people involved were relating to the elderly Rebecca. Even in her own mind she could not sort out what it all meant. . .or where it was heading.

Often in her daily devotions Becky prayed, *Lord, am I doing the right thing? Is it wrong for me to pretend to be Rebecca Sterling? Am I hurting anyone? Or is this the only way to uncover the truths You have for me? If I know my own heart, my only desire is to be of service to You and others. You have given me this unique opportunity. Let me use it to accomplish Your purposes. And, Father, whatever happens, please don't let me hurt Myrtle and Rand. I love them both!*

It was true. She had come to love these two very dear people. In her friendship with Myrtle, she was receiving much more than she gave. Myrtle was one of the wisest, most joyous women Becky had ever met. If only every young person could sit at the feet of such a gracious, accomplished lady!

And as for Rand, seeing him through the eyes of the elderly Rebecca made her love him all the more. The positive traits she had assumed he possessed were affirmed in the caring, loving way he related to his grandmother.

Since the night Rand had driven her home from Morning Glory, Becky had resolved to avoid him at all costs, at least while she was in disguise. That resolve lasted for several days— until the afternoon she entered Myrtle Watson's room and found Rand sitting beside his grandmother's bed reading her Bible. Myrtle was sound asleep.

Rand put his fingers to his lips. "I didn't want to disturb her, so I thought I'd just sit here and read until she wakes."

Rebecca lingered in the doorway. "I'll come back another time."

"No, please, come in!" Rand jumped to his feet and pulled the two overstuffed chairs side by side. "Here, sit down, Rebecca. We can chat until she wakes up."

Reluctantly Rebecca settled into the chair and pulled her bulky brown sweater close around her padded body. "I can't stay long."

"It's getting dark earlier. I'd be glad to drive you home."

"We'll see." Already Rand's closeness was causing little pitter-pats in her chest. Breathing through her latex mask was always a challenge, but Rand's disquieting presence stole what little breath she had. Feeling suddenly lightheaded, she put her head in her hands.

Rand leaned over and placed his palm over her gloved hand. "Are you feeling okay, Rebecca?"

"A little dizzy."

Rand got up and poured her a glass of water from Myrtle's pitcher. "I bet you walked all the way from your apartment, didn't you?"

She accepted the glass and sipped gingerly, careful not to dampen the latex around her mouth. "It's a fine day to walk."

"It's too far for a woman of your age. I told you to phone me."

"I'm not crippled yet." She hadn't meant to sound so defensive.

"Of course you're not. You're a very independent woman. And I admire that about you. But everyone needs help sometimes."

You've got that right. Someone get me out of here before I come unglued—literally and figuratively! Where are reinforcements when I need them? Rebecca cast a furtive glance at Myrtle slumbering contentedly in her bed. She was going to be no help today.

"How about a game of Chinese checkers while we're waiting?"

Before Rebecca could reply, Rand was already removing a large, flat box from Myrtle's closet shelf. He pushed the tray table over beside them and began setting up the game.

Rebecca was reluctant at first, but after a few minutes her competitive spirit surfaced and she found herself caught up in the game. She won the first one, Rand the second. As they played, their conversation ran the gamut—from the weather, Rand's classes, and Myrtle's health to the economy, Rand's childhood, and the conditions at Morning Glory.

"I know I can't expect this place to have all the niceties of home, but I do wonder if my grandmother is getting the proper care. She never complains, and everything looks satisfactory when I'm here. But what is it like when I'm not here?"

"That question has occurred to me too." Rebecca lowered her voice. "I've visited other residents. I've seen things that concern me."

Rand leaned his head close to hers. "What things?"

Rebecca hesitated, wondering how much she dared confide. "I've seen patients tied down to their beds. Attendants say it's to keep them from falling out, but it seems cruel to me. Some residents sit in their wheelchairs for hours without anyone coming near. I hear them cry sometimes. I try to console them, but there's so little I can do."

Rand closed his eyes and pressed his fingertips to his temple, as if in pain. "I dread the thought of my grandmother suffering like that."

"Whenever I come to visit, she seems content."

"Yes, she loves your visits. I'm so grateful to you, Rebecca."

"Don't be. Your grandmother blesses me more than I bless her."

Rand smiled. "You're a very wise woman."

She stared down at the game board. "It comes with age."

"I wish. . ."

She looked up. "You wish what?"

"Nothing really. I'm seeing someone. I wish she had your wisdom."

Don't go there, Rand! If you start talking about your beloved, self-serving Gloria, I'll explode! Her voice came out raspier than usual. "Your move."

He kept talking as he jumped four of her marbles. "Gloria is a beautiful, intelligent girl, but she doesn't understand me the way you and my grandmother do. She wants me to become a rich, successful attorney representing huge corporations and conglomerates."

"Is that what you want?"

"I wouldn't mind making good money. Who wouldn't? But it's not my priority. I love teaching. And I love my work with Legal Aid. I want to do all I can to protect the rights of the poor and underprivileged." He chuckled. "I know it probably sounds like pie-in-the-sky, silly idealism."

"Not to me. You sound like a very caring, generous man."

"It's not just me. I'm not naturally that altruistic. It's my faith. God has given me so much, and I believe He wants me to give back to others. Christ calls us to love others as He loves us."

She nodded. "I believe that with all my heart."

"I know you do, Rebecca." Rand reached across the game board and squeezed her gloved hand. "I hope you don't mind my saying this, but the women of yesteryear had a quality that's rare these days. I can't even define it. But I know it when I see it. You and my grandmother have it. Virtue. Integrity. Even a. . .a selfless nobility."

She shrank back, guilt settling like a rock in her chest. It was all she could do to find her voice. "You're being far too kind, Rand Cameron."

He laughed. "I'm sorry. It's the lawyer in me. I'm either waxing eloquent or spouting off like an idiot." He gazed back at the board. "Your turn, Rebecca."

Her fingers trembled as she made her play.

Rand followed with a clever move that ensured him the game. But his eyes were on Rebecca. "Do you have any advice for me?"

"Advice? No. You play Chinese checkers far better than I do."

"I'm not talking about the game. I'm talking about Gloria. I know she's waiting for me to propose marriage, but I'm not sure about her walk with God. She claims to be a Christian, but. . ."

Rebecca tightened her shawl around her neck and looked away. "I can't give you advice."

"But you must have some opinion."

Against her better judgment, she forced out the words. "Do you love her?"

Rand pursed his lips, then stared up at the ceiling. "I'm not sure. I guess I've never been in love or I'd recognize it."

A little flag of victory rose in Rebecca's spirit. "Then you have your answer."

"Maybe the more important question is, does God want Gloria and me together? How does a guy know when it's the Lord's will?"

"Do you pray together?" Where did that come from?

"No, we don't." Rand thought a moment. "Maybe I'll suggest it. If Gloria and I start praying together we'll grow closer spiritually. And maybe then I'll have my answer."

Rebecca lowered her wrinkled chin to her corseted chest. *Great! I've just begun giving advice to the lovelorn and sabotaged my own chance at romance!*

To her astonishment, Rand leaned over, slipped his arm around her shoulder, and planted a kiss on her forehead. "You're a remarkable woman, Rebecca. Generous, compassionate, kind, and wise." He looked her squarely in the eyes and winked. "If only you were fifty years younger, we'd make a perfect couple. Too bad I was born too late."

Rebecca steeled herself, her hands gripping the arms of her chair. It took every ounce of control she had to keep from ripping off her wig and confessing her true identity. *What am I going to do? This man is falling in love with the eighty-year-old version of me! How can the real Rebecca ever win his heart?*

&

The next time Rebecca visited Morning Glory, Myrtle's grandson was nowhere in sight. She felt a surge of conflicting emotions—relief that she wouldn't have to maintain her pretense before the man she loved and a pang of disappointment that they wouldn't have another special visit.

But all thoughts of Rand disappeared the moment Rebecca laid eyes on the pale, listless woman in the bed. The side rails were up. Myrtle looked small and helpless, her frail body hardly evident under the covers. Her hair hadn't been combed and she was still wearing her nightclothes. Surely this wasn't her dear friend with the bright eyes and ready smile.

As Rebecca approached the bed, Myrtle opened her eyes. "Rebecca, is that you?"

"Yes, Dear. Are you all right?"

Myrtle's eyes were glazed. "I had a bad night."

"What happened?"

"No one came to help me to the bathroom, so I got up by myself. I fell."

"I'm so sorry!" As she clasped Myrtle's hand, the elderly woman moaned. Rebecca's heart raced. "Are you hurt?"

"My wrists are sore."

"They're bruised!"

"They tied me down so I wouldn't get up again."

Hot, angry tears threatened to soak the latex around Rebecca's eyes. "Rand has to know."

"No, please, Rebecca. He has enough to do."

"He'd want to know."

"He would take me home."

"It would be better than this."

"I won't be a burden to him."

"He loves you, Myrtle."

"And I love him. Don't say a word, Rebecca."

"I can't promise."

Myrtle seized Rebecca's hand. "Most of the time this is a good place. I'm content here. I've lived my life. I want my grandson to be free to live his life too."

"Then I'll speak to someone here. They can't treat you like this."

Myrtle's eyes glittered with fear and desperation. "Don't make trouble. It won't happen again. I'll stay in bed until they come."

Rebecca turned away before Myrtle noticed her tears. "Did they check you to make sure you're okay? Did they take X-rays?"

"I didn't break anything. I would have known. I'll be fine."

"Just the same, I'm going to speak to someone. You rest, Myrtle, and I'll be right back." Rebecca clutched her cane and padded out of the room. She looked up and down the bleak hallway. Several residents sat bowed in their wheelchairs, but there wasn't an attendant in sight.

Rebecca plodded down the hall, her cane tapping a determined rhythm on the tile floor. Suddenly a male attendant emerged from one of the rooms and nearly toppled her with the full force of his burly frame. She fell back against the wall and steadied herself as he sidestepped her and kept going.

When she heard him mutter, "Watch out, old lady," she pivoted and struck him on the back with her cane. The blow wasn't hard enough to inflict pain, but it caught his attention. He whirled around and stared at her, as if to ask, How did you do that?

Leaning on her cane, she craned her neck up at him and glowered. "Are you the one who tied Myrtle Watson to her bed?"

His shaggy brows furrowed over his beady eyes. "Who wants to know?"

"I do. Did you tie her up?"

"Who are you?"

"Her friend."

"Yeah, I've seen you before. But you don't live here, do you?"

Rebecca's voice was fading to a squeak. "Answer me, young man!"

He broke into raucous laughter that shook his belly. "Sure, and I'll tie her down again if she gets out of that bed."

"You do and you'll regret it."

"You and which army are going to stop me?"

"I'll be watching you. If you hurt my friend again, I'll report you."

The man pointed a beefy finger at Rebecca. "Go ahead, old woman. Only nobody's listening. Nobody cares!"

Rebecca shivered as he swaggered off down the hall. Icy fingers of dread chilled her to the bone. She hugged herself but couldn't stop trembling. In the deepest part of her spirit she felt old. Worse, she felt helpless, invisible, demeaned. If this was what growing old was like, she wanted no part of it. But she had started something and had no choice but to see it through. She was in too deep to retreat, even if it meant walking through the valley of shadows to the very heart of death.

five

On the last Saturday of October, Lyn Orcutt stopped by Becky's apartment for an impromptu breakfast. Becky set a bowl of scrambled eggs, a plate of buttered wheat toast, and two glasses of orange juice on the small oak table in her sunny kitchen nook.

"Lyn, you want some boysenberry jelly?"

"Sure. It's my favorite."

"Mine too." She retrieved the jar from the refrigerator. "Sit where you like, Lyn. Not a lot of choices. Two chairs."

Lyn sat down. "Two is all we need."

Becky brought over the salt and pepper and sat down. "Will you ask the blessing, my friend?"

Lyn offered a brief prayer and closed with a petition for Becky's health and safety.

Becky smiled her appreciation. "You can tell by looking at me that I need prayer, can't you?"

Lyn reached across the table and patted her friend's arm. "To tell you the truth, Beck, you look awful. And I don't just mean the red splotches on your face from the latex. You've got circles under your eyes and your voice is scratchy. I think you're overdoing this whole old lady thing."

Becky stirred her eggs around her plate. "I don't know how to stop, Lyn. The truth is, my life as Rebecca Sterling is more compelling than my real life. Isn't that pathetic? She's become my life. I don't know who I am as Becky Chandler anymore. My whole identity is tied up in the old Rebecca. I think like her, I feel like her, I am her!"

"That's not healthy, Beck. You've got to finish your research and get back to your normal life."

Becky ran her fingers through her tangled curls. She hardly had time to take care of her hair anymore. "I've done the very thing I promised not to do—get emotionally involved with my subjects."

"Including Professor Rand."

"That's the greatest irony of all. You know how long I've adored that man from afar. I prayed for a chance to get to know him, to carry on a simple conversation with him. But nothing happened. . .until I became Rebecca Sterling. Now we've developed this wonderful bond. It doesn't matter that we're decades apart in age; this special, timeless connection ties us together in spirit."

Lyn's freckled brow furrowed. "Listen to yourself, Beck. You're not eighty, you're twenty-five. Rand Cameron is at least five years older than you are!"

Becky pushed her plate away. She wasn't hungry anymore, if she ever was. "What am I going to do, Lyn? I'm becoming schizophrenic! I find myself thinking like Rebecca Sterling. She's taken over my life, and I don't know how to get it back."

Lyn helped herself to more toast. "Simple. Kill her off."

"Kill her?"

"Not kill her literally. Just stop wearing the disguise. Let her quietly disappear."

Tears brimmed in Becky's eyes. This was crazy. She was weeping over someone who didn't exist. "The sad thing is that I'm a better person as Rebecca than I am as me. She's braver, kinder, more confident and compassionate than I could ever be. And she can carry on a conversation with Rand Cameron without clamming up like I do."

Lyn spooned up another helping of eggs. "You make it sound like she's an entirely different person. She's not. She's you, Beck. The best part of you. Whatever she is, you are too, if you'd just let it happen when you're in your normal skin."

Becky took her plate over to the sink and scraped the eggs into the disposal. "I'm not ready to let Rebecca go yet."

Lyn brought her plate over too. "Why not? Not enough research?"

"Unfinished business."

"With Rand?"

"With Myrtle. I've observed some things at the nursing home that bother me."

"What? Someone's pilfering cottage cheese off the lunch trays?"

"I'm serious, Lyn. I think some staff members are mistreating residents when no one's around to notice."

"You've seen this for a fact?"

"I've noticed some questionable activities." Becky filled the sink with soapy water. "I can't prove anything. That's why I want to take my pocket-size camcorder to the home with me."

"You're going to videotape the staff mistreating the residents? Isn't that a little extreme? Can't you just report them to the management?"

"What if the management doesn't care?" The brawny attendant's words still echoed in Becky's mind. *Nobody's listening. Nobody cares!*

"But it's not your responsibility, Beck. Contact the authorities, someone who's trained to handle that sort of thing."

Becky rinsed a plate and handed it to Lyn. "It would be my word against the home's. I've got to get proof."

"Why don't you talk to Professor Rand? It's his grandmother. Let him check into it."

"That's the problem, Lyn. When visitors and family members are there, the staff is on their best behavior. I want to record what happens when the residents are alone. Don't you see? I can walk around among them unnoticed because I'm one of them. The staff sees me as just another helpless old lady. I'm invisible to them."

"Invisible or not, it sounds risky to me, Beck. Evil people can be nasty when their wicked deeds are brought to light. You could be in danger."

"That's a chance I have to take."

They lapsed into silence as they finished washing and drying the dishes. Even with the sunlight streaming through the windows, the room felt darker, heavier somehow. When they had finished, Lyn set her dish towel on the counter and gave Becky a quick hug. "Please be careful, Beck. I have a bad feeling about this."

"Just keep praying, Lyn. I know God has a plan."

"I have a feeling you're talking about more than the problems at the nursing home. Do you think God has a plan for you and Rand too?"

Becky swished the dish towel over her ceramic countertop, then hung the towel on the rack. "I've never felt about anyone the way I feel about Rand. And the more we talk, the harder I'm falling. You have no idea how difficult it is to be near him, yearning for him to take me in his arms, and all the while he thinks he's talking to an eighty-year-old lady."

"Can't you find a way to break the ice with him in class now that you know him so well as the old Rebecca?"

They sat down again at the small kitchen table. "You would think so, Lyn, but I don't know where to begin. In class he's in his professorial mode. He sees all of us as just his students."

"Then maybe you should let him know who you are the next time you see him at the nursing home. Remove the disguise and tell him the whole story."

"In my mind I've done that over and over. I keep imagining different ways of breaking the news. But the time never seems right."

"Are you sure that's not just an excuse?"

"Maybe. I admit I'm scared. What if he hates me? What if his grandmother hates me too? I couldn't bear it."

"Pray about it, Beck. If God wants you to reveal yourself to Rand, He'll give you the chance."

Becky traced a water stain on the table. "I'm going to the home tomorrow. I plan to videotape any mistreatment I see. And if Rand is there, I'll tell him what I'm doing."

Lyn's grin turned her freckled face rosy. "You go, Girl!"

The next morning, as Becky applied her latex mask, slipped into her thick bodysuit and dowdy clothes, and adjusted her wig and pillbox hat, she was determined that this would be the day she would tell Rand the truth. Right after she got the video evidence she needed.

A half hour later, when Rebecca shuffled into Morning Glory Nursing Home, she was careful to keep her camcorder in the pocket of her flowing skirt. She greeted the nursing staff and attendants as she always did, with a meek nod and a raspy hello. Then, leaning on her cane, she hobbled off down the hall. Over the weeks she had made the acquaintance of many other residents besides Myrtle. Now it was time to visit them again, this time to videotape any signs of abuse.

Take your time, Rebecca. Don't raise suspicions. Be friendly and low-key. Look helpless as a lamb and harmless as a dove.

She stopped to visit Gertrude Smithers two doors down from Myrtle's room. Rebecca had seen her one morning with her hands tied down, but today she was sleeping soundly and her hands were free.

Rebecca tried the room across the hall, occupied by a wispy, smiling little man named Herman Frazier. He was sitting in his wheelchair watching television. In the past he had complained that no one helped him out of bed, but he seemed content enough now. Rebecca chatted with him for a few minutes, then journeyed on.

As she approached a room at the end of the hall, she heard a commotion—a man growling orders and a woman wailing. Rebecca recognized the voice of Maria Sanchez, a stout little lady with olive-black eyes, who usually greeted Rebecca in Spanish. The man's voice was all too familiar too—the hefty attendant who had nearly knocked Rebecca down in the hall.

Rebecca inched closer to the partly open door, her pulse quickening. Now she could see inside. What she saw stunned her. The man was holding Maria down and tying her wrist to the bed rail. "Hold still, you old biddy, or you'll be sorry!"

Maria was sobbing. "Por favor, no. I will be good. Don't hurt me!"

Rebecca struck the door with her cane. The man whirled around and stared at her with a mixture of surprise and contempt. "Go away, old woman. We're busy!"

She squared her shoulders, aimed her cane at the attendant, and in her most grating voice declared, "I came to see Maria."

He hesitated, as if weighing his options. Finally, with a menacing glare, he released Maria's wrist and threw the cord on the bed. "I'll be back later."

He stormed out the door past Rebecca, then turned around and looked back at her. Something in his expression unnerved her, but she forced herself to remain steady under his hostile gaze. "You're quite the busybody, aren't you?"

"I'm just visiting a friend."

"And I'm watching you. Don't forget it!"

Rebecca didn't move until the man had disappeared down the hall. She couldn't move. Her legs were trembling. For the first time since posing as an octogenarian, she was thankful for her cane. She might have collapsed without it.

She spent the next half hour sitting by Maria's bedside, comforting and reassuring her, and listening as Maria poured out her woes and fears in Spanish.

When she left Maria's room, she wrestled with a sense of

helplessness and anger. *Lord, how can I help these poor people? What can I do? I'm just one person. Whether I'm Becky or Rebecca, who is going to listen to me? How can I prove the things I've seen? Maybe it's time to take Rand into my confidence and see what he can do.*

As she headed for Myrtle's room, the thought of Rand brightened her spirits. Perhaps he would be there today visiting his grandmother. Maybe she would be able to end this bizarre masquerade now. She would take Rand aside and tell him everything. Finally he would see her as the person she really was. He would know that Becky and Rebecca were one. And if he cared about the elder Rebecca, perhaps he could care for the young Becky as well.

But when she entered Myrtle's room, her spirits sank. Rand wasn't there. There would be no unveiling today.

Fighting her disappointment, Rebecca greeted Myrtle with a gentle embrace, then settled into the chair by the bed. She was relieved to see her friend looking so well—sitting up in bed, wearing a pretty blue smock, her hair combed, and a dab of rouge on her cheeks.

"You look lovely today, Myrtle. Is this a special occasion?"

The feeble woman flashed her expansive, sunshiny smile. "My grandson is coming. He said he has a surprise."

Rebecca's heart surged. So Rand would be there after all. It wasn't too late to put her plan into effect. "When will he be here?" It didn't really matter. She would wait.

"When will who be here? If you mean me, I'm here now!"

Rebecca swiveled in her chair and looked up in anticipation as Rand stepped through the doorway. As he smiled at her, a tickle of pure happiness spiraled up her spine. It was all she could do to keep from pulling off her mask and disclosing her real identity. Once he knew her secret, perhaps they could begin building a relationship based on truth.

"I told you I had a surprise, Grams."

"Yes, I remember, Dear. What is it?"

Rand stepped back into the hallway and returned holding a woman's hand. It was Gloria Farrington, looking fabulous in a cotton candy pink designer dress and three-inch heels, her blond hair swept back in a French twist.

"Grams, this is the girl I've been telling you about."

As Rand made the introductions, Gloria remained several feet from the bed, clasping her small handbag.

Myrtle was all smiles. "I'm so pleased to meet one of Rand's friends."

"It's great meeting you too, Mrs. Watson. Rand talks about you all the time."

"Don't listen to a word that boy says, unless it's good, of course."

"Every word he says about you is good."

Myrtle patted Rand's hand. "That's my boy."

Rand looked over at Rebecca and brandished his infectious grin. "And, Gloria, this is Rebecca Sterling, a friend of Grams', and a good friend of mine too."

Rebecca nodded, forcing herself to remain composed, outwardly serene. But inside her skull, warning bells and whistles were going off like crazy. This was the last place she wanted to be—in the presence of Rand's ravishing, self-absorbed sweetheart. At last she managed a squeaky, "How do you do?"

Gloria offered a tight smile and remained where she stood. "Nice to meet you, Miss Sterling."

Rand started to pull a chair over for her, but she waved him off. "I've been sitting all day, Darling. I don't mind standing."

Rand took the chair himself, then leaned over and clasped his grandmother's hand. "I've been wanting you and Gloria to get acquainted for months now. Isn't she just as I described?"

"Lovely. A sight for sore eyes."

Rand smiled at Rebecca. "And what a treat. I get to introduce Gloria to two of my favorite gals. Rebecca, you remember me mentioning Gloria, don't you?"

Rebecca kept the reproach from her voice. "Indeed, I do." *This voluptuous blond is my worst enemy! How can I compete for the man I love in a frizzy wig, dowdy dress, and padded, sagging body?*

Rand's exuberance was expanding. "Gloria, this little lady and I are kindred spirits. We think so much alike, it's scary."

"How nice for you." Gloria gazed around the room with the critical eye of someone watching out for cockroaches. "We can't stay long, Rand."

"We just got here."

Under her breath Gloria murmured, "It smells bad in here, Rand."

"Not that bad."

"You're just used to it."

Annoyance thickened his voice. "In a minute you'll be used to it too."

Gloria hugged herself defensively. "I don't want to get used to it."

Rand sprang from his chair, took Gloria's arm, and led her over to the window. Although they spoke in hushed tones, Rebecca could hear every word. And surely Myrtle could too.

"I told you I wanted us to spend a few minutes with my grandmother."

"We did. And now it's time to go."

"We haven't finished our visit."

"Yes, Darling, we have. You promised to take me to lunch."

"I will when I'm good and ready."

Gloria flounced to the door. "Whether you leave or not, I'm getting out of this creepy-crawly place." Her words hung in the air, brittle as icicles.

Myrtle spoke up, her voice a bit too bright. "Rand, Dear,

you run along with your beautiful lady. She's right. This is no place for you young people to be."

Rebecca winced, seeing Rand torn between two loyalties. But he wasn't ready to give up yet. He stopped at the doorway and turned to Rebecca. "Would you like to join Gloria and me for lunch?"

She shook her head, speechless.

"We'd love to have you. Wouldn't we, Gloria?"

Gloria wrapped her arm around Rand's neck. "Darling, let's go."

"What about it, Rebecca? Will you go to lunch with us?"

"Can't you see, Rand, Darling? She doesn't want to go."

Rebecca lowered her head, humiliation creeping over her like toxic fumes. She could feel Gloria's loathing and Rand's pity enveloping her, suffocating her, sapping the very lifeblood from her soul. She had never felt more useless and degraded. "Another time, Rand. I'm sorry." She was sorry for so much more than a missed lunch. She regretted that they had grown so close as soul mates and yet remained worlds apart.

To her surprise, Rand slipped over, bent down, and kissed her cheek. "Another time then, Rebecca. I'm not going to let you get away that easily."

Tears smarted in her eyes as Rand followed Gloria out the door. Their voices echoed in the corridor, Gloria's strident, Rand's muffled. And then there was silence. Rebecca gazed around Myrtle's room and shivered with a sudden sense of desolation. Pressing her gloved fingers to the wrinkled cheek where Rand's lips had touched, Rebecca vowed never to put herself in such a humiliating situation again. From this day on she would avoid Rand at all costs, even if it meant staying away from Morning Glory and doing her research somewhere else. Even if it meant giving up her cherished friendship with Myrtle and Rand forever.

six

Through the first week of November the elderly Rebecca Sterling made no appearance at the Morning Glory Nursing Home. Only twice during that week did Becky don her disguise and venture out as an octogenarian—once to the nearby shopping mall and once to downtown Las Rosas. Neither trip proved eventful. Becky's heart wasn't in it anymore. She considered compiling the data she had gathered so far and writing her dissertation just to be done with it. It wouldn't be the stellar work she had imagined, but at least she could put behind her the emotional turmoil her elderly persona had generated in her own heart.

On a Saturday afternoon, as Becky sat at her computer entering data, the doorbell rang. She considered ignoring it. She was on a roll and any interruption would slow her momentum. But the caller was persistent, so after the fourth ring, Becky got up and headed for the door. Under her breath she muttered, "Whoever you are, I'm in my grubbies and up to my elbows in work!"

She peered through the peephole and spied a tall, broad-shouldered man in a leather jacket and jeans. His back was to the door, but there was something familiar in his stance. Then he turned and rang the bell again. His face was all too familiar. Professor Rand Cameron—in the flesh! Becky's heart palpitated with disbelief. *What's he doing here?*

Becky leaned her back against the door as if somehow that would keep her caller at bay. She was trembling, her mind misfiring wildly. She couldn't think straight. *What do I do? Pretend I'm not home? But I have nothing to hide. He doesn't know I'm Rebecca Sterling. It could be nothing. Or maybe it's about Myrtle. Maybe she's ill.*

Becky pushed back her tousled hair and smoothed her tailored shirt over her stretch jeans. She inhaled sharply, then gripped the doorknob and with a decisive flick of her wrist swung open the door. Flashing her most welcoming smile, she crooned, "Professor Cameron! What a pleasant surprise!"

He stared down at her as if he had seen a ghost. "Becky?"

"Yes, of course." This was weird. He was clearly more surprised than she was.

"Becky Chandler?"

His bafflement peeved her. "Yes, that's me."

"From Sociology 304."

"Second row, third seat from the left. What brings you here, Professor?"

He looked around as if trying to get his bearings. "I was looking for a friend of my grandmother's. I was sure this was where she lived."

Becky's mouth went dry. "A friend of your grandmother's?"

"She's a good friend of mine too. Rebecca Sterling. I brought her home one evening. I was sure this was her apartment."

Becky licked her lips, but it didn't help. "This. . .this is the place."

Rand leaned closer. "Pardon, I didn't hear you."

She forced herself to meet his gaze. *Might as well spill the beans. He's going to find out anyway!* "I'm Rebecca Sterling Chandler."

A curious smile played on his lips. Finally light dawned in his eyes. "Really? I didn't know."

She stared at the ground, shame warming her cheeks. "I should have told you sooner. It's a long story."

"No problem. I'm just surprised your grandmother didn't tell me."

"My grandmother?" Becky was beginning to think she

was at the Mad Hatter's birthday party. Nothing was making any sense.

"Your grandmother and I have become good friends, Becky. I thought she would have told me her granddaughter was in my class." His blue eyes crinkled in that special way that made her heart do flip-flops. "Surely she's told you about me."

Becky wrung her hands. "I don't know how to answer that."

He laughed. "Don't worry, I won't put you on the spot." He gazed past her into the apartment. "Is your grandmother home?"

Becky stepped back inside the door. "I–I'm the only one here."

"Oh, well, I'm sorry I missed her. But that's good news, I guess."

"Good news?"

"If she's out somewhere, she must be well. I was worried about her."

"Why?"

"She hasn't visited my grandmother for awhile. We were both afraid something had happened to her. With someone her age, you never know."

Becky nodded. "What about your grandmother? She's okay, isn't she?"

"Sure. You can't keep the old girl down. She's marvelous."

Becky couldn't hide her relief. "I'm glad. She's a wonderful person."

Rand winked. "So your grandmother has told you about us."

Becky managed a coy smile. "I've learned a little about you, that's true."

Rand stepped closer, his gaze moving over her face with a scrutiny that unsettled her. "I see it now. The heart-shaped face, the same mouth and eyes. Even the same smile."

He knows! Closing her eyes, Becky gripped the door to keep from swaying. "I hope you'll let me explain."

"Explain what? That you're the spitting image of your grandmother? You should be proud. You have a wonderful legacy in her."

"I know." This paradoxical conversation was more than Becky could bear. She looked back yearningly at the safe little world of her apartment. She never would have dreamed she'd want to escape the attentive gaze of Professor Cameron, but at this moment it was all she could think of. "Excuse me, Professor. I'd better get back to work."

He made no move to leave. "What are you working on?"

"My doctoral dissertation. It's due the end of the semester."

"Really? I'd like to hear about it."

She gaped at him. *Sure, now you want to hear about it! Where were you when I tried to work up the courage to get your advice?*

Rand looked at his watch. "How about the two of us going out for coffee? Then you can tell me all about your dissertation."

"I really can't."

"Maybe I can give you a few pointers. I've graded quite a few dissertations in my time."

She looked down at her clothes. "I'm not dressed for anywhere fancy."

He gave her an approving glance. "You'd look good in anything."

That compliment did it. "I suppose I could take a few minutes."

"Great. There's a coffeehouse a few blocks from here. The Bermuda Bistro."

"It's one of my favorite places."

"Perfect! I'll wait for you in the car if you want to take a minute to freshen up."

"Thanks. I'd like that."

She dashed back inside, ran a brush through her chestnut curls, applied some makeup, and changed into an embroidered

V-necked shirt and drawstring pants. *At least now I look like a girl instead of a ragamuffin!*

Rand smiled as she slipped into the passenger side of his car. "Five minutes! I'd say that's some kind of transformation. You look terrific!"

"I didn't want people to think I was your charity case."

"No way."

As Rand drove, Becky gazed around his automobile, remembering sitting in this very seat as the elderly Rebecca. Even though their conversation had been sweet, her disguise had set up an invisible barricade between them. She was old, he was young. That was a barrier neither could cross. But now, age was no longer a deterrent. They were both young and free and full of life and limitless possibilities. She could feel his admiring gaze on her. She sensed he was as attracted to her as she was to him. The sensation was heady, exhilarating.

He glanced over at her. "You're awfully quiet. But then that's your nature, isn't it? I've seen you struggle to speak up in class."

She gazed at her hands. "I don't know why I get so tongue-tied. I'm not always so shy. I lead a high school Bible study and have no problem as long as I have my notes. But when I'm winging it, I just can't seem to get the words out."

"I teach a sixth grade boys' Sunday school class, and they really keep me on my toes. Sometimes their questions stop me dead in my tracks, and I just have to ask God to give me the words."

"That's the only way I can speak before a group. I throw myself on God's mercy and tell Him He's got to do it because I can't."

"And He always comes through, doesn't He?"

"Always. But as often as I've asked Him to take away my shyness, it's still there. I guess it makes me rely on Him all the more."

"Nothing wrong with being shy, Becky. You know the old saying, 'Still waters run deep.'"

She laughed. "I never did know what that meant."

"Me neither. But it sounds good."

Minutes later he pulled into the parking lot of the Bermuda Bistro, an aging, nondescript building nestled between a bank and a dry cleaning establishment. "As you know, it doesn't look like much, but their food and coffee are great."

"I know. My friend Lyn and I come here all the time."

"Is that your boyfriend?"

She smiled. "No. Lyn's a girl. We grew up together in Seattle."

"And you both escaped the rain and cold weather to come here?"

"Something like that."

Rand came around and opened her door. "Since they have such good food here, we could make it an early dinner."

"It beats putting in a TV dinner at home."

As they crossed the parking lot, she noticed he kept his hand on her elbow. She loved walking beside him—his physical closeness, the feeling that they were together, a couple. And his touch on her arm was electrifying.

This has to be a dream. But if it is, don't wake me up!

As if sensing they wanted privacy, the hostess seated them at a table in the back corner, away from the hubbub and commotion at the front. A ballad was playing, something moody and familiar, with a hint of country. The ceiling lights cast a rosy glow on the oak table, accentuating the warmth and conviviality of the place. As Becky sat down across from Rand, she felt absolutely giddy. *Wait 'til I tell Lyn about this! She'll never believe it!*

The waitress was already taking Rand's order. "I'll have the prime rib sandwich." He turned to Becky. "What looks good to you?"

She thought of saying, It's not on the menu, but she caught herself and said instead, "The spinach quiche."

"And two coffees," added Rand.

When their food was served, he removed his glasses and slipped them into his shirt pocket. "May I ask the blessing?"

"Please do."

He offered a simple prayer, but it was the most beautiful Becky had ever heard. Praying with the man she loved was even more wonderful than she had imagined.

As they ate, she studied his sturdy face—the way his blue eyes crinkled when he smiled, his habit of rubbing his chin when he was serious or pushing back a lock of ebony hair from his forehead when he was amused. She had observed these traits as the elderly Rebecca, but somehow they seemed more intimate to her now. She wanted to know more—the kinds of things a man would tell a woman about himself. But she had to be careful not to reveal how much she already knew. It would be a fine balancing act, but she was up to the challenge. Never had she felt such confidence and euphoria.

Rand leaned toward her. "Becky, you're smiling. Am I missing something?"

Her cheeks flamed. "I'm having fun. Thanks for inviting me."

"I'm glad I did. I can't believe you're the same girl I can't coax a word out of in class." He sipped his coffee. "And you're Rebecca Sterling's granddaughter as well. It's a small world!"

"Smaller than you know."

"We should have invited her!"

"Who?"

"Your grandmother. Surely she's home by now. Give her a call."

Becky swallowed hard. "I really can't do that."

He nodded. "You're right. This is better, isn't it? Two's company, as they say."

Her face felt flushed. "Wonderful company."

"We have a lot in common, Becky."

"You think so?"

"Our grandmothers, for one thing. You understand what I'm dealing with."

"I do?"

"Of course. You live with your grandmother. The two of you must be very close."

She lowered her lashes. "Closer than you think."

"People sometimes needle me for being the devoted grandson. Gloria does. She doesn't understand it."

"Gloria?" Becky failed to keep the iciness out of her voice.

"She's a friend of mine. You've probably seen her. The tall blond. She drops by my classroom from time to time."

"She doesn't like your grandmother?"

"She won't give herself a chance to get acquainted."

Becky focused on her quiche. "That's a shame."

"Sometimes I think she's jealous."

"Surely she knows why your grandmother is so important to you."

Rand searched her eyes. "You know, don't you?"

"I know—I heard—your grandmother raised you."

"Do you know the whole story?"

"I'd love to hear you tell the story." *Again,* she added silently.

Almost to the word he repeated what he had told the elderly Rebecca about his parents dying in a car crash when he was eight and his grandmother raising him. But he didn't stop there. As he turned his coffee cup between his palms, he drifted into dark and distant memories. "I was this scared little boy who couldn't understand why his parents had been taken away from him. My whole world had been turned upside down. I was so angry with God."

She touched his hand. "That must have been so painful."

"It was. The summer before, I had accepted Jesus as my Savior in vacation Bible school. After the accident, I blamed

Jesus. I refused to go to church. But my grandmother was patient with me. She kept saying, 'Just tell Jesus how you feel. Don't stop talking to Him, no matter what.'"

"A very wise woman."

"One day she caught me crying." Rand's eyes glinted with unshed tears. "In my anger I had crushed a model car my dad had made me. I stomped on the thing until it was toothpicks. So there I was sitting on the floor trying to put it back together and yelling at the top of my lungs how mad I was at God."

"What did she do?"

"She picked me up, tucked me in the crook of her arm, and let me cry." Rand's voice broke. He brushed his hand over his eyes. "Then she told me to tell Jesus how I felt. So I did, haltingly at first; then I got into it and poured out all the dark, ugly feelings. When I was done, my grandmother said, 'Jesus loves you just the same. He's weeping right along with you. When you hurt, He hurts.'"

"Your grandmother is a profound woman."

"I'll never forget the next thing she said. 'Honey, if you can get hold of the fact that Jesus loves you even when the worst thing happens to you, you'll make it through this life. He may not take away the bad things, but He'll walk you through them. And He'll weep with you and hurt with you and never let you go.' Then she looked me in the eye and said, 'Even though you're angry, I have a feeling you still love Him, so why don't you tell Him so?' That was the day my faith became real."

Becky blinked back her own tears. "That's one of the most beautiful stories I've ever heard."

"And it's all true. My grandmother had such amazing faith. She had just lost her daughter and son-in-law, and yet she was concerned about me and my walk with God."

"No wonder you're so devoted to her."

He sipped his coffee, then held the cup between his palms.

"The hardest thing now is the prospect of losing her. That day is coming soon, and I dread it. My grandmother has been my rock, my consolation, my encourager, my hero. . . And the thought of living without her is painful." He grimaced. "I don't know why I'm telling you these things. I'm not usually this talkative."

"I feel honored."

"I guess it's because you remind me so much of your grandmother. I have strong affections for that dear lady." He chuckled. "I don't know what it is with me and old people. Frankly, I'd rather spend time with them than with most people my own age."

Becky nodded. "I've felt that way myself. Old folks I've known have gained such wisdom and grace. I admire them immensely."

"Me too. Folks like our grandmothers. Yet people shut them out of their lives. They don't listen to them, don't value their opinion. It's absurd how we view old people. We should be sitting at their feet gaining every bit of knowledge we can. They've managed to navigate this turbulent world successfully. They have stories to tell, so many fascinating experiences to share. And yet people of our generation devalue them and want nothing to do with them. I'd give anything to change things."

"So would I." Becky's heart stirred with a sudden, delicious exhilaration. Here was a man who shared her vision of the elderly. No wonder she loved him so much! She steadied her voice to camouflage her excitement. "Our generation not only ignores old people, we discriminate against them. That's what I intend to show in my dissertation."

"Tell me more about this dissertation of yours."

She told him as much as she dared, with one glaring omission. She couldn't bring herself to tell him that she was Rebecca Sterling.

They talked on for another hour. When Rand finally looked at his watch, his brows shot up in amazement. "I can't believe the time. I promised my grandmother I'd stop by an hour ago."

"I'm sorry. I rambled on far too long."

"Not at all. I'm glad you told me about your research. I hope you'll let me read your dissertation when it's finished."

"I'd love to."

Rand looked at the check and tossed several bills on the table. Then they both stood up and faced each other. He took her hand between his palms. "We'll have to do this again soon, Becky. I've enjoyed it."

"Me too."

He smiled and scratched his head. "Like I said, I've never bared my soul like this to someone your age. You're very much like your grandmother. Not just your physical features, but your personality as well. You have her generous, caring heart, and her decency and integrity."

"There's a reason for that, Rand." *If I don't tell him the truth now, I might never find the courage!*

He grinned. "Good genes, I suppose. And good upbringing."

"There's more." She was trembling now. "It's a long story."

He took her elbow and urged her toward the door. "Can we save it for our next date? I really need to see my grandmother before she thinks I've dropped off the face of the earth."

Her resolve crumbled. "I suppose so."

As he drove her home, Becky's heart did emotional flip-flops. The door was opening for a relationship with Rand Cameron, but would her deception destroy their love before it even had a chance to blossom?

seven

Over the next two weeks of November, as brisk winds and falling temperatures seized the California coastline, Becky felt springtime budding in her heart. Twice Rand Cameron had taken her to dinner at the Bermuda Bistro and once to a university concert. Several times they met for lunch at the campus cafeteria. And one afternoon they drove to the ocean and walked along the beach, swapping nostalgic memories and funny stories, confiding secret hopes and gossamer dreams. They had become friends, good friends.

But, so far, nothing more than friends.

Still, for Becky, it was a beginning, a wonderful, unexpected adventure that held the promise of romance. She was well aware that Rand was still seeing Gloria as well. Several times he mentioned her and invited Becky's opinion, never apparently noticing the chill that settled between them at the mention of Gloria's name.

Only twice during those two weeks did Becky venture out as the elderly Rebecca, and then only to gather more evidence of abuse at the Morning Glory Nursing Home. Both times she stopped in to see Myrtle Watson, who welcomed her with hugs and tears. During her second visit, the day after Thanksgiving, Rand Cameron arrived with red roses for his grandmother.

When he spotted Rebecca, he beamed. "Miss Sterling! Or should I say Mrs., now that I've met your granddaughter?"

"Just Rebecca, please."

He handed her one of the roses. "It's good to see you again! It's been a long time, Rebecca. How are you?"

Her impulse was to bolt and run, but she forced herself to remain in the overstuffed chair beside Myrtle's bed. As she accepted the rose, she mumbled under her breath, "I've been staying close to home."

Rand laid the bouquet in his grandmother's arms, then sat down at the foot of her bed, facing Rebecca. "I don't blame you for staying home. The weather's turned cold. You should stay in where it's warm."

Myrtle lifted her roses to her nose and inhaled deeply. "These are gorgeous, Rand. But what's the occasion?"

"Just to say I love you, Grams."

Myrtle looked at Rebecca. "Isn't he wonderful? You'll have to take half of the roses with you. I don't need them all."

Rebecca shook her head. "One is enough for me."

Rand leaned closer to Rebecca. "How is your granddaughter?"

"My granddaughter?" Rebecca's fingers tightened around the stem. A thorn pierced her glove. She winced.

Rand raised his voice. "Your granddaughter, Becky. Surely she's told you about our visits."

Rebecca had half a mind to pull off her wig and be done with this maddening masquerade. But what if the shock gave Myrtle a stroke? She was trapped in her own terrible, unwitting invention. "Yes, I'm aware of your visits."

Rand smiled beguilingly. "I hope you approve."

This is crazy! I've got to get out of here before I become totally schizophrenic! "I do approve! You're a fine young man."

He folded his hands, his expression solemn. "I suppose you're wondering about my intentions."

Intentions? Don't take me up that road! Spare me! "Let's not discuss intentions, dear boy. It's not my business."

"Of course it is. You're her grandmother."

The implications of Rand's words took root. Rebecca craned her neck toward him. "You have intentions, young man?"

Rand chuckled as if she had said something funny. "Not

intentions really. Becky and I are just friends. But I do have questions. . ."

"Questions?"

"I'm not saying this very well."

Myrtle piped up. "What my grandson is trying to say is that he's quite smitten with your granddaughter, Rebecca, and he doesn't know what to do about it."

Rebecca sat back in her chair, dazzled. She couldn't quite catch her breath.

"Now look what you've done, Grams. You've left Rebecca speechless."

"Well, someone had to tell her you have designs on her granddaughter."

Rand raised his hands in self-defense. "Not designs. That sounds contemptible."

Myrtle traced a rosebud with her arthritic fingers. "You've talked about nothing else for two weeks, Rand."

"All right, I admit I'm quite taken with her. She's very much like you, Rebecca. I'm sure that's your doing."

At last Rebecca found her voice. "I. . .I can't deny that."

"The problem is, Rebecca, I'm not quite sure how to handle things."

Warning lights flashed in Rebecca's brain. "What things?"

"Everything. The truth is, I'm seeing two women. I hadn't planned it that way. And I care for them both. Gloria has been in my life nearly forever, but I've kept her at a distance. I wasn't ready for anything serious. But now there's Becky. You can see the predicament I'm in."

Rebecca seized her cane and hoisted herself out of her chair. She couldn't endure this bizarre conversation for another minute. "I must go."

"No, please, not yet." Rand sprang from the bed and helped Rebecca back into her chair. "It's such a quandary. I really need a bit of advice."

"I can't—"

"Just tell me this. Has Becky mentioned me?" He sat back on the bed. "Of course, she's mentioned me. I don't doubt that. But has she said anything specific? Anything important? You know what I mean."

Rebecca's throat constricted, parched as a desert. She barely managed to utter, "I don't remember."

Rand's countenance fell. "You remember nothing she said?"

"She. . .she doesn't say much."

"Perhaps I've assumed too much."

On impulse, Rebecca tapped Rand's knee with her long-stem rose. "No, you haven't assumed too much." *If I'm not careful, I'm going to shoot myself in the foot!* "She is very fond of you. She thinks you are a wonderful man." *There! I've said it! Will I live to regret it?*

Rand grinned from ear to ear. "She said that?"

Rebecca sank back in her chair. "That, and more. Much more."

"Tell me."

With a flick of the wrist, Rebecca waved her rose at him. "Talk to her. Not me. Tell her how you feel."

Rand nodded. "You're right, of course. You're a wise woman, Rebecca."

Not wise enough to keep myself out of a jam like this!

Rand got up, enveloped Rebecca in his strong arms, and planted a kiss on her cheek. "I'm going to let you ladies visit, while I go make a phone call. Is Becky home right now?"

Think fast, Beck! "No, she's out. But she'll be home this evening."

Rand paused in the doorway. "I almost forgot to ask. Did you and Becky have a nice Thanksgiving?"

"Very nice."

"I thought she might have gone home to see her parents."

"They live in Seattle. She wanted very much to see them,

but she didn't have the money to fly home. And there wasn't enough time to drive."

"That's too bad. Maybe I can take her out this weekend and cheer her up."

Rebecca tried to keep her smile in check. "That would be a very nice gesture indeed."

❧

Sure enough, Rand phoned Becky that evening and invited her to have lunch with him on Saturday. When he mentioned that he had seen her grandmother at the nursing home that afternoon, she replied, "Yes, I know," and changed the subject. As much as she wanted to spend Saturday with him, the thought of keeping the truth from him another day was intolerable.

As soon as she had gathered sufficient proof that residents of Morning Glory were being mistreated, she would abandon her disguise forever.

On Saturday, after a leisurely lunch at the Bermuda Bistro and a brief walk on the chilly, windswept beach, Rand suggested that he and Becky drop by the nursing home. "I can't believe you haven't met Grams yet. Our grandmothers are such good friends. It's time for the two of you to get acquainted."

"I–I'm not sure that's a good idea," Becky stammered as he walked her to his car.

"Nonsense. It's an idea whose time has come. Grams will love you."

Will she? Or will she guess I'm keeping a terrible secret from her and her precious grandson?

Becky's palms were perspiring and her head began to ache as Rand escorted her into his grandmother's room a half hour later. The shades were drawn and Myrtle Watson was sound asleep. Relief swept over Becky until she noticed how pale and feeble Myrtle looked. Rand turned on the bedside lamp and kissed the slumbering woman on the cheek.

"Rand, don't disturb her. She probably needs her rest."

"You're right. We'll come back another time."

As he snapped off the lamp, Myrtle stirred and gazed up at him. "Rand, Dear, is that you?"

He leaned over the bed and took her hand. "Yes, Grams. I've brought a surprise. Your friend Rebecca's granddaughter."

"Rebecca?" Myrtle turned glazed eyes toward Becky. "Thank you for coming, Dear."

Becky took a tentative step toward the bed. "Hello, Mrs. Watson. I'm glad to meet you."

Myrtle stretched out a trembling arm, thin as a twig, and clasped Becky's hand. "Rebecca, dear Rebecca."

"It's Becky, Grams. Rebecca's granddaughter."

Time to change the subject. "Are you feeling okay, Mrs. Watson?"

Myrtle laid her head back on the pillow, her gray hair a bird's nest of tangles. "I'm feeling a bit under the weather today."

"What's wrong, Grams? Can we do something for you?"

"I didn't sleep well last night."

Rand's voice rose with alarm. "Were you ill?"

"No. I. . .I tried to get up."

"Grams, you know better than that. You've got to let someone help you."

"I rang. But no one came. I waited and waited, until I couldn't wait any longer." Her voice dissolved into a whimper. "I didn't want to soil my bed."

Rand folded her hands in his. "So you got up by yourself, Grams?"

"I tried. The attendant came and scolded me. He tied me down so I wouldn't get up."

Becky met Rand's gaze and saw anger and frustration kindling in his eyes. Gently he examined his grandmother's hands and arms. "Your wrists have bruises. I'm going to have a doctor check you out."

She seized his hand. "No, Rand, I'm fine. They'll be angry if you complain."

"Let them be. They can't treat you this way!"

"I shouldn't have disobeyed. Next time I'll stay in bed. I'll be okay."

Rand removed his hand from his grandmother's and tucked the covers around her frail body. "You rest, Grams. I want to have a word with the nurse on duty." He gave Becky a knowing glance. "Keep an eye on her. I'll be right back."

Before Becky could reply, Rand strode from the room, a man with a mission, not to be deterred. She heard him moments later in the hallway speaking to someone. His voice was low and urgent while a woman's voice came back quiet and conciliatory. The night nurse, no doubt—a pleasant, likable woman Rebecca had met before. Most of their conversation was muffled, but bits and pieces came through.

"It's outrageous to tie her down like a common criminal."

"It's for her own good. She could fall. Break her hip."

"There has to be a better way."

"We'll look into the matter, Mr. Cameron."

"Just see that someone comes when she calls. Immediately, not a half hour later."

"We do our best, Mr. Cameron."

"It's not good enough."

"We do what we can, considering we're overworked and understaffed."

"Then perhaps I should take this up with your supervisor."

"Perhaps you should, Mr. Cameron."

While they talked, Becky sat in the chair beside Myrtle's bed and held her delicate hand. Myrtle's eyes were closed, but a smile flickered on her thin lips. "It's good to have you with me, Rebecca. You never fail me."

Becky answered in her natural voice. "It's good to be with you too, Myrtle. I love you."

Myrtle nodded, still smiling. "I know you do, Dear. I love you too."

After a minute, Rand returned, his face animated with a vivid intensity. Becky had never seen him look more disturbed. He moved across the room to Myrtle's bed with a nervous agitation, his gestures too sharp, too abrupt, as if he couldn't quite keep his emotions in check. And yet, as he sat down, he offered Myrtle his most expansive grin. "It's going to be okay, Grams. The nurse promised to come right away when you ring for her. But you let me know if they give you any more trouble, and I'll box their ears."

Myrtle nodded. "I'm sure everything will be fine now, Dear."

Rand stood. Tentatively, he brushed Myrtle's wispy hair back from her forehead. "We're going to let you get back to sleep, Grams. I'll be here to see you tomorrow."

She patted his hand. "Good night, Grandson. Good night, Rebecca."

Becky brushed a kiss on Myrtle's forehead and whispered, "Sleep well, my friend."

Rand was silent as he drove Becky home. It was a troubled silence, one she was reluctant to intrude on. What could she possibly say to reassure him about his grandmother? There was no easy answer. He couldn't care for her himself. Where else could she go? Uprooting her and sending her to another nursing home would just confuse and upset her. And who was to say one nursing home would be better than another?

Besides, how could Becky offer Rand advice when she had her own worries and misgivings? She had a feeling Myrtle recognized her tonight. It was baffling and inexplicable, but somehow Myrtle knew she was the elderly Rebecca. If Myrtle knew, she would likely tell Rand. Whatever happened, Rand had to hear the truth from Becky herself. The truth coming from anyone else would surely decimate their fledgling romance.

As Rand drove through the narrow, darkened streets toward her apartment, she silently practiced ways of telling him about her masquerade. *Funniest thing, Rand! You'll never guess what I've been doing. . . . It's all for research, and I meant to tell you, but the subject never came up. . . . I hope you're not upset, but I've been living a double life. . . . You know how fond you are of my grandmother? Well, guess what! My grandma is me!*

The more she played the various scenarios over in her mind, the more she realized she was in too deep to salvage the situation. A man of great character and faith like Rand Cameron would not take being lied to and made a fool of lightly. If she valued his friendship, she couldn't reveal the truth to him. . .ever!

eight

On Monday morning, when Becky knew Rand would be busy teaching his class, she donned her disguise and went to visit Myrtle at Morning Glory. The frail woman was sitting up in bed finishing her breakfast, and there was a hint of color in her cheeks. The shades had been raised and sunshine spilled into the room. It seemed a much different place from Saturday night.

When Myrtle saw Rebecca in the doorway, she smiled and held out her hand. "Dear friend, so good of you to come by so early."

Rebecca shut the door behind her, then shuffled across the room, her cane tapping a staccato beat on the linoleum. She kissed Myrtle's cheek, sat down in the chair beside the bed, and adjusted her pillbox hat on her silky mound of gray hair. "I hear you weren't feeling well Saturday night, Dear."

Myrtle sipped her coffee, her knobby fingers wrapped around the mug. Her hands shook as she set the mug back on the breakfast tray. "I'm better today. The nurse helped me up in the night."

"I'm glad to hear that."

"You were here, weren't you? Saturday night? Wasn't that you?"

Rebecca's heart hammered and her mouth went dry. She couldn't form a response. Couldn't quite breathe. *Lord, don't let me mess this up now when I have one last, important thing to do before the elderly Rebecca disappears forever.*

Myrtle paused, her forehead crinkling, as if she were trying

76

to decipher a puzzle. "Or was that your granddaughter? She's so like you. I thought it was you."

Rebecca leaned close to the bed, trying to quell the pounding in her chest. "Does it matter, Myrtle? You know I am your friend, don't you?"

"Yes. My good friend."

"I care about what happens to you."

Tears glistened in Myrtle's eyes. "I know you do, Dear."

"Your grandson cares too. He's worried about you."

Myrtle's pale lips quivered. "I know. The poor boy. I don't know what to do."

"I know, Myrtle. But I have an idea."

"You do?"

Rebecca lowered her scratchy voice to a whisper. "I want you to listen to me very carefully. I have a plan."

"A plan?"

"I believe some people here have not treated you well. Is that so?"

Myrtle's expression shifted, her eyes and mouth drooping with shame and dismay. "True."

"But we can't prove it, can we?"

"No, we can't. No one listens to me. No one believes me."

"Myrtle, what if we could prove it?"

"How?"

Rebecca slipped her pocket-size camcorder from her roomy handbag. "If you're willing to help me, we may be able to videotape anyone who mistreats you."

"You want me to take pictures of them?"

Rebecca pointed to the framed console on the wall. "I'm going to hide this camera next to the TV. It will be aimed at your bed. And I'm going to give you a remote control device like you use for the television set. But this one will turn the tape on and off. Do you think you can handle it?"

Myrtle looked baffled, concerned. "How will I know when to turn it on?"

"Start the camera whenever you ring for help. If you're treated well, then we'll simply rewind the tape and no harm is done. If someone abuses you, we'll have it on tape, and I'll give it to the proper authorities."

Myrtle raised her hands to her puckered lips. "Oh, Rebecca, I'm afraid. What if someone finds out?"

"No one needs to know. It's our secret. If you are being hurt, others are being hurt as well. We need to catch the abusers and make sure they never hurt anyone again. So will you help me, Myrtle?"

She nodded, a tear crossing her wrinkled cheek as she reached for her Bible on the nightstand. She clasped it to her chest. "God is our strength. He will help us in times of trouble."

"Yes, Myrtle. He will never leave us or forsake us. If we trust in Him, He will help us."

They were both silent for a long moment. Then Rebecca got up and quietly carried her chair across the room. After a sidelong glance at the closed door, she hoisted herself up on the chair and maneuvered the camcorder between the television set and the framework. It would be undetectable unless someone were looking for it. Lifting the folds of her flowing skirt, she stepped back down and gave a sigh of relief. So far so good. No one had entered and caught her executing her little subterfuge. Now if Myrtle could carry out her part of the plot, Rebecca's plan just might bear fruit.

After showing Myrtle how to work the remote control, Rebecca kissed her friend good-bye and slipped out of the nursing home before anyone noticed her. She drove back to her apartment, changed out of her disguise, and showered. There was nothing more she could do now but hope and pray she could gather enough evidence to bring about drastic changes at Morning Glory. *It will be worth having lived two lives if I can make things better for those dear people.*

As she applied moisturizer to her tender, reddened face, she studied her reflection in the bathroom mirror and thought about the merry-go-round she had been on for the past few months. *My skin can't take much more of that latex mask. And I can't take living like this anymore. I don't know who I am. I look at myself and see a stranger. Which Rebecca am I? All I wanted to do was help the elderly and carry on authentic research for my dissertation. So why do I feel so trapped and guilty? Why do I feel like I'm hurting and deceiving the people I care about most? Somehow everything has gone terribly wrong, and I don't know if I can ever fix it or get my life back again. All I know is, if I value my own sanity, I've got to get rid of Rebecca Sterling once and for all!*

But that was easier said than done.

As she applied her makeup, her spirits lifted as she watched the youthful Rebecca appear. This was who she was. She couldn't let the elderly Rebecca play with her mind anymore. Rebecca Sterling Chandler was young and carefree and full of life, with her whole future ahead of her. And now it was time to go to class—Rand's sociology class—and focus on the pivotal events of her own life, especially her growing friendship with Rand. She vigorously brushed her hair until golden highlights glistened in her loose chestnut curls. She slipped on a citrus-orange top, earth-toned striped pants, and a light khaki jacket. Oh, the simple, delicious pleasure of feeling attractive again!

As she drove to class, she mulled over what to do with her alter ego, Rebecca Sterling. Should she just toss out all the paraphernalia—the wigs and clothing and makeup—she had amassed to create Rebecca? It would be easy enough to discard the outer trappings, but how could she scour the person of Rebecca from her own heart and soul? Was she obligated to tell Rand about her bizarre experiment, or could she simply let Rebecca fade away into obscurity without another word to anyone?

Guilt jabbed her conscience as she contemplated keeping her secret from Rand. The plain truth was, no matter how she disposed of her elderly persona, she had to tell Rand everything. Scripture said to speak the truth in love. She owed him the truth, even if it shattered their blossoming relationship. "I'll tell him today, after class," she vowed as she pulled into the campus parking lot.

She had her chance after class when Rand dismissed the other students but motioned for her to stay behind. "Becky, do you have some time to talk?"

"Now?"

"No, I have classes all afternoon. I was thinking about tonight."

"Tonight? That would be. . .fine."

"Are you free for dinner?"

"Free? Yes, I'm free. Definitely free."

"Good. I have something to talk to you about."

"Something important?"

"I think so."

A warning signal flashed behind her eyes. Had Myrtle told him she was Rebecca? Surely not. Myrtle had mentioned how much the two were alike, but that didn't mean she knew the truth. Or did she?

Becky steadied her voice. "Where shall I meet you? The Bistro?"

"No, let's step up a notch. Do you know that little Italian restaurant on Fourth? Antonio's?"

"Yes, I've been there once or twice."

"Great food and friendly atmosphere. Shall we meet there at seven?"

A tickle of pleasure went through her. "Sure. Seven sharp."

He squeezed her arm, a special light in his eyes. "See you tonight."

She was nearly walking on air as she headed outside to the parking lot. Nothing in the professor's demeanor had suggested he was angry with her. Just the opposite. *He cares about me! I can see it in his eyes. Hear it in his voice.*

She was almost to her car when she heard footsteps behind her. She turned and stared into the glowering face of Gloria Farrington. Wearing a formfitting dress and stiletto heels, her blond hair in its customary French twist, Gloria leveled Becky with her stony gaze.

"I have some advice for you, Miss Chandler."

Becky attempted a reply, but no sound came forth.

"Stay away from Professor Cameron. Don't interpret his attentions as anything more than the dutiful charity and goodwill he would give any student." With her manicured hands on her swiveling hips, Gloria took a step closer and tapped one stylish shoe on the pavement. "You're only making yourself a laughingstock when you follow him around like an eager little puppy dog. Do yourself a favor and find some guy in your own league. The professor is taken."

Before Becky could reply, Gloria Farrington turned on her spiked heels and flounced off.

When Becky met Rand at the Italian restaurant that evening, she debated whether to tell him about her unsettling encounter with Miss Farrington. Surely he'd want to know how rude and cruel the woman could be. *Or would he think I'm behaving badly by tattling on her? Lord, what is the right thing to do? Give me Your wisdom and compassion. And give me the courage to tell Rand about my posing as Rebecca Sterling before this infuriating masquerade spoils everything between us.*

They were halfway through dinner before Becky decided against mentioning her run-in with Gloria. Bad-mouthing

Gloria would accomplish nothing except to stir up trouble and cast Becky herself in a negative light. Better for Rand to discover for himself what Gloria was like. That left the other issue—telling Rand the truth about disguising herself as an octogenarian.

Mentally rehearsing what she would say, she twirled a strand of spaghetti around her fork. *Rand, I hope you don't think less of me for what I'm going to say. I haven't been quite myself lately. Actually, I've been two people. . . .*

"Becky, are you going to eat that spaghetti or turn it into a ball of yarn?"

She stared at him, bewildered. "What?"

He grinned. "You've been swirling that same spaghetti on your fork for ten minutes now."

"I have?" She popped the mound of pasta into her mouth and chewed self-consciously. "I'm sorry. My mind was somewhere else."

"Obviously."

She swallowed hard. "It's just that I have something important to tell you."

"What a coincidence."

She raced on before she lost her courage. "I know how much you value the truth, Rand. So do I. But sometimes a person gets caught up in something, and it snowballs, and before you know it, you're in too deep to back out."

"Exactly." He forked up a slice of pepperoni from his antipasto salad. "That's what I want to talk to you about."

"You know what I'm going to say?"

"No, I know what I'm going to say. May I go first?"

She shrugged. "Be my guest."

"This isn't easy to explain. It's about Gloria."

"Yes, I've met Gloria."

"It's never been serious between us. We've been friends, much as you and I have been friends."

Becky groaned inwardly. She didn't like the sound of this. Was he going to tell her he was marrying Gloria? Please, no! "You don't owe me any explanation, Rand."

"Maybe not, but it's important to me to keep everything aboveboard in my relationships. Honesty is vital. Without it, you have nothing."

Becky squirmed. This wasn't going well at all.

Rand speared a morsel of lasagna. "I've been honest with Gloria about our friendship—yours and mine—just as I've been truthful with you about my relationship with her."

"And I appreciate that, Rand, but, like I said, you don't owe me anything. We're friends. And you have a right to have other friends."

"Becky, let me finish."

She lowered her gaze, duly chastened. "I'm sorry. Go on."

He ate the lasagna, then wiped a bit of tomato sauce from his mouth with his linen napkin. "It's like this. . . . I've been doing a lot of thinking."

Becky folded her hands in her lap to keep from trembling. *He's nervous. He's actually nervous! What terrible thing is he going to tell me?*

"The truth is, Becky, I've told Gloria there can't be anything but friendship between us."

"Between you and me?"

Rand's brows shot up. "No, I mean between Gloria and me."

"Oh." Hope rose in Becky like a white dove in flight.

"Becky, I told her I intend to pursue a relationship with you."

"With me?"

"If you're willing to take our friendship to the next level."

A delicious warmth spread through her face and neck. "The next level would be nice."

"Then it's settled. I'd like to consider you my girl."

"What did Gloria say when you told her?"

"She was quite reasonable. She wants to remain friends."

Gloria's snarling voice echoed in Becky's head—Stay away from Professor Cameron! "Rand, if you don't mind my asking, what went wrong between you and Gloria?"

"I suppose I do owe you the whole story. I don't want there to be any secrets between us, Becky." He inhaled sharply. "It was Gloria's duplicity that made me realize there could be no future for her and me."

Becky winced with sudden guilt pangs. "What did she do?"

Rand focused on his lasagna for a moment, his brow furrowed. Finally he looked up with shadowed eyes. "Gloria led me to believe she shared my faith in Christ. Oh, I knew she didn't have the same interest I had in spiritual things, but I thought her faith would deepen as she grew in the Lord. I'm not saying I expected her to be a saint. Or maybe I did expect too much, I don't know."

"Are you saying she's not a believer?"

"She admitted she's been going to church just to please me. She doesn't have a clue what a real relationship with Jesus is like. I tried to tell her last night, but she said she's tired of keeping up the pretense, of trying to be someone she's not."

Becky sank down in her seat. *Dear Lord, he could be talking about me! I'm tired of trying to be someone I'm not too. What will Rand say when he finds out both the women in his life have been deceiving him?*

"Becky, don't look so troubled. I'm glad I know the truth about Gloria."

"You are?"

"Yes, because now I know she's not the one for me. Oh, she tried to persuade me to compromise my standards. She said she was willing to let me go to church if I was willing to let her stay home. But I told her I'll have none of that. The woman I marry has to be wholeheartedly committed to the Lord. She has to be authentic and genuine and deeply in love with Jesus. She has to be someone sincere and transparent like you, Becky."

Like me? Oh, Rand, your flattery condemns me! Heat spread across Becky's face and neck and left her palms sweaty. Her stomach knotted. The spicy aromas of garlic and oregano were suddenly too heavy in the close, airless room. She yearned desperately to jump up from the table and run away, to escape Rand's puzzled scrutiny. But she sat paralyzed, her ankles too weak to carry her.

Rand reached across the table for her hand. "Becky, I'm sorry. Maybe I'm speaking out of turn. Forgive me if I'm assuming things that aren't there. Maybe you have no interest in me except as a friend. If that's the case, just tell me so, and I'll respect your wishes."

Fighting lightheadedness, she sucked in a reviving breath. "It's not that, Rand. I just feel. . .a bit dizzy. It's awfully warm in here."

"Would you like to go?"

She rubbed her forehead. "Maybe some fresh air would help."

Rand signaled their waiter. "Check, please."

Within minutes he had paid the bill and ushered her outside into the brisk night air. He slipped his arm around her waist as he walked her to his car. "Feeling better?"

She nodded. "I don't know what hit me."

"I hope you're not catching the flu."

"No, I'll be fine." At his car, she turned to face him. "See? The cold air is reviving me."

"Good. You had me worried."

She looked around. "I'd better go. I drove my own car."

"I know. But I'm not letting you leave until I'm sure you're okay."

She managed a wan smile. "All right, Dr. Cameron. What's your diagnosis?"

The streetlamps cast Rand's handsome features in sharp lights and shadows. Even in the darkness, his eyes glinted with tender concern. Gently he cupped her face in his strong hands. "No fever. You must be on the mend."

She smiled, warming to his touch. "I'm getting better by the minute."

Their gaze held for a long while, neither of them speaking. Finally, as if in slow motion, he bowed his head to hers and sought her lips. The kiss was warm and tender, like the brush of velvet on her mouth. She hoped it would last forever.

When at last he released her, she struggled to find her voice. "Rand, I have to tell you. . ."

"What, dear girl?"

"The truth. . ."

"The truth?"

"About my grandmother."

"Your grandmother?"

"I've tried to tell you so many times. . . ."

He broke into raucous laughter. "Sweetheart, we've just shared the most marvelous kiss. I'll remember it forever. Please, let's not break the enchantment of this moment by talking about your grandmother."

Her eyes grew teary. "You don't understand."

He brushed a tear from her cheek. "I do understand. I love the old girl dearly, but there's nothing I want to know about her tonight."

"But, Rand—"

He silenced her with a kiss.

nine

"Lyn, I am a total wimp!"

It was the first Saturday in December. Lyn and Becky were decorating her artificial blue spruce with the tiny, twinkling white lights. Neither of them had their mind on the tree.

"No, you're not a wimp, Beck."

She unwrapped a silver garland and handed one end to Lyn. "Yes, I am. I'm a sissy-faced coward."

"You just haven't found the right time to tell him."

"The right time? Are you kidding? I should have told Rand the truth the first time I met him as the old Rebecca. I should have said, 'Professor Cameron, you'll never believe it, but this is your sociology student under all this latex and padded bodysuit.' Then he and his grandmother never would have formed such an attachment to Rebecca Sterling."

Lyn wound the garland around the tree's spiky branches. "It's not too late, Beck. You'll see."

"What do I do? Wait until Rand and I are sending out our wedding invitations and say, 'Oh, by the way, don't bother sending one to my grandmother. She doesn't exist.'"

"Wedding invitations? This is more serious than I thought."

"That's a bad example. I'm exaggerating. Fantasizing. It'll be a miracle if Rand even speaks to me once he finds out the truth."

They both stepped back and scrutinized the tree with its lopsided garland. Lyn unwrapped it and they started over. "Rand will understand, Beck. You were never trying to deceive him. Your intentions have been honorable all along."

"That's true. Rand and Myrtle are so fond of Rebecca

Sterling. I couldn't just blurt out the truth without hurting them."

"Absolutely." They wound the garland around the tree again.

"Then why do I feel so guilty? Why do I feel like I've committed some horrible transgression? Why do I feel like a liar and a cheat?"

"Maybe because doing something wrong for the right reasons is still wrong?"

Becky handed Lyn a glass ornament. "Thanks a lot. Whose side are you on anyway?"

"Yours, Beck. This whole thing started out as an accidental misconception." Lyn hung the ornament on the tree and reached for another. "But the longer it goes on, the more you have to cover your bases to keep from spilling the beans. I guess you're right. You have no choice but to divulge the whole improbable story as soon as possible."

Becky reached up and placed a shimmery angel on the treetop. "And if Rand never speaks to me again?"

"If he's the man you think he is, he'll forgive you. Maybe he'll even be amused."

"That's wishful thinking."

"Would you like to spend a few minutes praying about it?"

Becky nodded. "Would you do the honors?"

They put aside the tree trimmings and sat down together on the sofa. Lyn put a consoling hand on Becky's arm. "Heavenly Father, we thank You for loving us so much that we can come to You with any problem. Please help Becky know what to do and give her the courage to do it. Help her find the words to explain to Professor Cameron why she was impersonating an elderly lady. Please let him be understanding and forgiving. And if Professor Cameron is the man you have chosen for Becky, let everything work out so they can be together. In Jesus' name."

Together they said, "Amen."

Lyn looked back at the half-decorated tree. "Looks like we'd better get back to work, or it's never going to look like Christmas around here." They spent another hour finishing the tree and setting up a manger scene on the coffee table. Lyn placed a festive green and gold wreath in the front window beside the door. "Now it's starting to look like Christmas!"

Becky stepped back and surveyed their handiwork. Yes, her modest apartment glowed with a lovely holiday charm. "Now I'll have to come over to your place, Lyn, and help you decorate."

"What about tomorrow?"

"I need to become the elderly Rebecca at least one more time so I can check on Myrtle Watson without raising suspicion."

"Just be careful. If someone is abusing the residents, who knows what they might do to someone who's on to them."

Becky nodded. "This is something I have to finish, Lyn. My job isn't done until I know Myrtle Watson and the others in that home are safe."

Lyn gave her a reassuring embrace. "My prayers are with you, my friend."

❧

The next morning, as Rebecca arrived at Morning Glory, she was thankful for Lyn's prayers. As she hobbled down the hallway to Myrtle's room, she had an uneasy feeling someone was watching her. Someone was suspicious. She paused and rested on her cane, feigning weariness. Glancing around, she patted her gray hair and pulled her shawl tighter around her padded frame. *Must be my imagination. I'm getting paranoid in my old age.*

As she started back down the hallway, a blur of movement caught her eye—someone stepping out of a doorway directly into her path. She stopped just short of colliding with the tall, burly man. Steadying herself with her cane, she stared up into the dark, glaring eyes of the attendant who had been suspicious of her before. She was close enough this time to read his identification badge. His name was Dirk—Dirk Seuer—and he eyed her with enough contempt to make her cower.

He placed his beefy paw on her shoulder. "Going somewhere, old woman?"

Squirming away from his touch, she managed a raspy, "Just on my way to visit my friend, Myrtle."

"Myrtle Watson ain't up for company today."

Alarm bells sounded in Rebecca's mind. "Is she ill?"

"Let's just say she didn't have a very good night. Why don't you come back tomorrow, lady."

"No, thank you. Myrtle will need some cheering up, so I'd best mosey on to her room." With pounding heart, Rebecca sidestepped the stony-faced attendant and pressed on, praying that he wouldn't resort to physical action to restrain her. *If he manhandles me, he'll get my handbag alongside his head!*

The man stepped aside and let her move on down the hall. *Keep your pace natural and unhurried,* she cautioned herself, *with just a bit of tottering in your gait. Don't let him think he rattled or intimidated you. And don't let him ever suspect you're not a harmless old lady!*

When Rebecca entered Myrtle's room, she was surprised to see the shades drawn and Myrtle still asleep. It was nearly ten. Surely someone should have brought her breakfast by now. *Do I dare wake her or just let her sleep?*

Rebecca slipped over to the bed and gazed down at her dear old friend. Even in repose, Myrtle's wrinkled face showed such strong character and grace. What a remarkable lady! Rebecca was fortunate to have Myrtle Watson as a friend.

An unexpected emotion passed through Rebecca like a chill wind in the dark—a profound sense of sadness and loss. She shivered, shaken by the surprising power of her feelings. What was this nameless pain that twisted in her soul? Yes, of course. She was already grieving the end of her friendship with Myrtle. For surely, when she gave up her disguise, she would miss their special times together. The two of them had connected in a way only two people of the same generation could bond.

Then it struck Rebecca that her grief went deeper than losing her friendship with Myrtle. Giving up her own identity as the elderly Rebecca would be like experiencing a death. Improbable as it seemed, she was grieving the demise of a person who didn't exist. How strange was that?

And yet the old Rebecca did exist. The young Rebecca had created her and made her a part of her very being, a side of her personality she hated to relinquish. To excise her now would mean leaving an empty place in her heart. She would miss the old Rebecca as much as she would miss Myrtle.

"Rebecca, is that you?"

Rebecca jumped, startled, but quickly composed herself. "Yes, Myrtle. You were sleeping. I didn't want to disturb you."

Myrtle made a low, moaning sound. "It's so dark."

"I'll open the blinds." Rebecca crossed the room and raised the shades. A wintry sun washed the room with pallid light. "Is that better?"

Myrtle raised up on one spindly elbow. "My arm hurts."

Rebecca approached the bed. "Did you fall in the night?"

"No."

"Did you try to get up by yourself?"

"I couldn't."

"Did they tie you down?"

"I think so."

"They tied your wrists to the bed?"

Myrtle sounded fretful. "I. . .I couldn't move."

Rebecca examined Myrtle's wrists. They looked a bit bruised, but not enough to cause her pain. "Where does it hurt, Myrtle?"

"My arm."

As Rebecca pushed back the cotton sleeve of Myrtle's

nightgown, she saw the source of her complaint. A large, purplish bruise stood out on her white skin like an ink blot on paper. "Oh, Myrtle, what happened to you?"

"I tried, Rebecca, but I couldn't walk."

"Because you were tied down."

"No, they untied me."

"Who?"

"I don't remember."

Rebecca smoothed back Myrtle's mussed hair with her gloved hand. "Try, Dear. It's important. Start from the beginning. Tell me exactly what happened last night."

"I woke and rang the call bell. Someone came to help me to the bathroom. But my legs wouldn't work well."

"Did you fall?"

"No." Myrtle's eyes filled with tears and her thin lips quivered. "I couldn't move fast enough, so he. . .he hit me."

Rage and indignation flared in Rebecca's chest, but she forced her voice to remain calm. "Who hit you, Myrtle?"

"I don't remember."

"Was it a nurse? An attendant? Surely you know who it was."

Myrtle looked at her with pleading eyes. "Maybe I was dreaming. Maybe it didn't happen at all."

Rebecca clasped Myrtle's hand. "I understand. You're afraid. But, whoever it is, we can't let him hurt you again."

"I tried to hurry, but my legs wouldn't carry me."

"Myrtle, that's no excuse for someone to hit you." Glancing up at the hidden camcorder, Rebecca whispered, "Did you start the videotape before you rang the call button?"

Myrtle lowered her lashes, shamefaced. "I forgot."

Rebecca stifled her disappointment. "It's okay. Tonight I'll come back and start the recorder before you go to sleep. We'll get a good six or eight hours of tape. If anyone bothers you tonight, we'll have him."

When footsteps sounded in the corridor, Rebecca fell

silent. A nurse breezed through the doorway with a breakfast tray—a stout, dark-haired woman Rebecca hadn't seen before. "Good morning, Mrs. Watson," she crooned. "You were sleeping earlier, so I saved your meal for you." She glanced over at Rebecca. "Oh, I see you have company."

"I'm Rebecca Sterling." Resting her weight on her cane, Rebecca sized up the woman. Middle-aged, round face, pleasant smile, honest eyes. . .

As the nurse gave Myrtle her tray, she cast a sidelong glance at Rebecca. "Are you a resident here too, Miss Sterling?"

"No, just visiting my friend."

"Would you like some hot tea or apple juice?"

"No thank you. I can't stay long." Rebecca read the woman's name badge. Selena. An idea was brewing. Did she dare enlist this woman's help? "Selena, may I ask you a question?"

"I suppose."

"How long have you worked for Morning Glory?"

"One week today."

Rebecca beckoned her over with a gloved finger. "May I ask a favor?"

The woman shrugged. "What is it?"

Rebecca lowered her voice confidentially. "My friend Myrtle has bruises on her wrists and arms. Do you have any idea how they got there?"

Selena looked at Myrtle's arms. "Older people bruise easily. You've probably noticed that in yourself, Miss Sterling. Bruises, age spots, skin discoloration. It's a natural part of the aging process."

Rebecca's ire was rising. She had to remind herself to stay in character. "Those aren't natural bruises or age spots."

Selena examined Myrtle's arms more closely. "Do you try to get out of bed by yourself, Mrs. Watson?"

"Sometimes."

Selena looked over at Rebecca. "They probably had to use

wrist restraints to keep her from climbing out of bed and falling. Better a few bruises than a broken hip."

Rebecca wasn't mollified. "Myrtle said someone hit her last night. Do you know anyone on staff here who would do such a thing?"

Selena's eyes grew wide as saucers. "I'm sure no one here would lay a hand on a resident. This is a very reputable establishment, Miss Sterling."

"I'm sure it is, but there are bad people everywhere, and at least one of them is here at Morning Glory."

Selena's voice turned chilly. "I don't know who it would be."

"Neither do I." Rebecca lowered herself into the chair by Myrtle's bed. She felt suddenly as old and spent as the woman she was portraying. "Would you do one thing for me, Selena?"

"If I can."

"Keep an eye on Mrs. Watson. Check on her at night. Make sure she's okay."

"Sure. Whenever it's my shift, I'll look in on her."

"Thank you. I'd appreciate it."

Rebecca left shortly after that, feeling drained and disheartened. She would stay in character today since she would be visiting the home tonight to start the camcorder. Her efforts were likely to prove futile, but what more could she do? She would try one last time to get proof of the abuse against Myrtle. Then, whatever evidence she had, she would take to the management at Morning Glory and, if necessary, to the authorities.

Meanwhile, she would return to her apartment and begin the painful process of expunging the elderly Rebecca from her life forever.

ten

Rebecca returned to her apartment that afternoon with an ache in her chest nothing could dispel. Already she was grieving for herself and for Myrtle, for the friendship that would end tomorrow, and for her inability to improve Myrtle's living conditions.

When the idea to disguise herself as an octogenarian had first seized her imagination, she hadn't anticipated the emotional toll it would take. She had created a person who had formed strong emotional attachments with others—especially with Rand and Myrtle—and now it was time to let go.

But could she?

Even as she went through her closet gathering all the vestiges of the elderly Rebecca—thrift shop dresses, shawls, support hose, and padded undergarments—she wasn't sure she could relinquish her alter ego. At last she sat down on her bed with an armload of Rebecca's stuff and broke into tears.

"Lord, I've handled things so badly," she said between sobs. "Why didn't I just focus on my research? Why did I let Rebecca form emotional connections that have to be broken now? I'm hurting the very people I care most about. But if I tell them the truth, I'll hurt them even more."

It was true. She was trapped in a dilemma of her own making and had no idea how to disengage herself without making things even worse.

Burying her latex-covered face in one of Rebecca's old wool sweaters, she thought about Rand and the many times she had almost told him her secret. What had kept her silent? Fear! Fear that he would reject her and think less of her, that he would condemn her for maintaining her masquerade for so long. She wasn't willing to risk their blossoming relationship by divulging the truth.

But if she couldn't tell Rand the truth about her impersonation of Rebecca Sterling, what chance did she have to build a deep, abiding connection with him? And if he learned she hadn't been honest from the beginning, how would he know for sure he could ever trust her?

Setting the bundle of clothes aside, Becky got up and gazed at her reflection in the dresser mirror. The elderly Rebecca stared back solemnly. Becky's tears had caused the latex around her eyes to separate from her skin, giving her face an odd, accusing grimace.

"Great! Now I'll have to reapply my mask before going to the nursing home tonight." It was a task she didn't relish. Her skin was already red and tender. Maybe she should forget about returning to the home to turn on the camcorder. How likely was it that the videotape would pick up anything of significance anyway?

If she didn't go, would she be forsaking Myrtle in her moment of greatest need? The question needled her and spawned even more guilt. She yanked off her wig and pillbox hat and threw them on the bed. "Why should I feel so responsible for Myrtle Watson anyway? She's not my grandmother. She got along fine before I met her, and she'll do just fine without Rebecca Sterling in her life. She has Rand. He's the one who should be watching out for her, not me!"

Even as she said the words, arguments assailed her mind. *Myrtle puts on a happy face for her grandson. She doesn't want him to worry about her. Only with her friend Rebecca has she been candid about the abusive treatment she's received. God put her in your life for a reason, Becky. Don't abandon her now.*

With a sigh of resignation, she gingerly peeled the latex off her forehead and cheeks. "Guess I'll have to put all this goop back on tonight for my visit to Morning Glory. Then I'll have just one more time to step into character. . .tomorrow when I pick up the camcorder in Myrtle's room."

Becky had just finished moisturizing her face when her phone rang. She was surprised to hear Rand's voice. "Are you busy tonight, Becky?"

"Busy?" She stalled. "I'm not sure. What did you have in mind?"

"I need your help. I want to go shopping and buy my grandmother a Christmas tree for her room and some gifts to put under the tree. I thought you and your grandmother might like to come along and give me some advice."

Becky sank down in the nearest chair. "You want my grandmother and me to go shopping with you?"

"If you can both make it. Your grandmother knows Grams better than just about anyone. I bet she can come up with all sorts of gift ideas."

Becky's mind raced. She said the first thing that came to her. "I'm sorry, Rand. She spent the morning at the nursing home with your grandmother. I don't think she's up to another excursion today." *What are you saying, Becky? You're digging yourself in deeper!*

"Oh, sure, I understand. Tell her how much I appreciate her visits to the home. They're the highlight of my grandmother's days."

"That's sweet of you to say, Rand."

"So then it'll just be the two of us tonight."

"The two of us?"

"You and me. I can't do this alone, Becky. Shopping is not my forte."

"I'm not sure I can go, Rand. There's something I have to do."

"Oh? I thought you said you were free."

"I. . .I said I wasn't sure."

"Grams will be disappointed."

"You're visiting your grandmother? I thought you were just going shopping."

"I was hoping the two of us could go shopping and then take the tree and gifts over to the home tonight."

Becky brightened. If she went to the nursing home as herself, she could turn the camcorder on before they left. She would have to do it without Rand noticing. But surely it would be better than having to put on her disguise again. "On second thought, Rand, I'd love to go shopping with you. And take a tree and gifts to your grandmother."

"Terrific. How about I pick you up around five and we can grab a bite to fortify us for the holiday crowds."

"I'll be ready."

As she hung up the phone, excitement pumped through her veins. She was going to spend the evening with Rand! The very thought of his closeness made her mind reel. And what a bonus. She would be able to turn on the camcorder and fulfill her obligation to Myrtle as well.

There was only one fly in the ointment. Or maybe two. She had just told Rand a deliberate lie, further compounding her tangled web of deception. It would be that much harder now to tell him the truth. Would she find the courage to tell him tonight? And what about Myrtle? Would Becky rouse Myrtle's suspicions with another visit as herself?

These questions and more plagued her as she stuffed all the evidence of the elderly Rebecca into two paper bags—the makeup and wigs, the shoes and hats, the sweaters and skirts, the spectacles and gloves. She kept out just one outfit for her final appearance tomorrow at Morning Glory when she would retrieve her camcorder. The rest of the paraphernalia would be carted off by the Good Will truck. And to be sure she didn't change her mind, she phoned for a pick up in the morning.

Becky's mood improved as she showered for her date with Rand. An impromptu evening with the man she loved was almost too good to be true. She took extra care with her hair and makeup and slipped into her favorite corn silk cardigan and floral print skirt. She always felt a bit like a time traveler when she removed the trappings of old age and became a young, attractive woman again. She could feel her very personality change as she gazed at the youthful woman in the mirror. Even her body felt different—lighter, more energetic and alive, as if by sloughing off the old Rebecca, she could suddenly scale mountains or run races or even fly.

And tonight, with Rand by her side, she would be flying indeed!

He arrived at five sharp, and his sweeping gaze told her everything. Here was a man in love! "You look incredible, Becky. I don't know what you're doing to yourself, but you look better every time I see you."

Her pulse quickened. "You look pretty good yourself."

He was wearing khaki slacks and a black turtleneck sweater that accentuated his broad shoulders, and his thick dark hair curled over his ruddy forehead in the casual, meandering way she adored.

He stepped inside and kissed her cheek. "Or maybe you look so good because my feelings for you grow stronger every day."

She smiled, her face pleasantly warm. "Why, Professor Cameron, I had no idea you were such a sweet-talker."

He matched her smile. "You haven't seen anything yet." He offered her his arm. "Are we ready to go?"

She grabbed her handbag and a light jacket. "I'm ready if you are."

He looked around. "Shouldn't we tell your grandmother we're leaving?"

She nudged him out the door. "No, that's not necessary."

He drove her to Antonio's, where they shared a pepperoni pizza and antipasto salad. Already it had become their special place. In a cozy booth, with a cheery backdrop of candlelight and Christmas carols, they reminisced about Christmases past.

"When I was a little boy, before my parents died, my dad used to dress up as Santa and pretend to come down the chimney. I'd be in bed, too excited to sleep, and I'd hear all this noise outside. Then I'd hear a knock and I'd run to the front door, and there was Santa, complaining about being too big to fit down our chimney. So, of course, I'd invite him in for milk and cookies, and he'd give me my presents to put under the tree until morning. My heart would be pounding so hard, because how many kids got to entertain Santa in their own living room?"

Becky laughed. "I wish I could have seen you then."

"The last time or two he played Santa, I was seven, and I began to notice that this bearded old fellow looked an awful lot like my dad. But I didn't let on because my dad was having such a good time, and I wasn't about to spoil it."

"Were you angry with him for deceiving you?" The question held greater weight than Becky cared to admit.

"Angry? No, not really. But I was disappointed. I had really believed I was entertaining the great Santa Claus himself. When I realized it was my dad, I didn't feel quite so special anymore. But later, after my dad died, I cherished those memories. I was thankful my father had loved me that much."

Becky helped herself to another slice of pizza. "Christmas was always my favorite time of year. Every year we used to go to my grandparents' home just outside Seattle."

"Your Grandmother Sterling?"

Her throat tightened. "Yes. I would always sing that old song, 'Over the river and through the woods—' "

" 'To Grandmother's house we go. . .' Yes, I sang that song too." Rand took the last wedge of pizza. "Your grandmother is such a plucky lady, I bet you had a ball at her house."

"Oh, yes. She did Christmas right. Everything—the food,

the decorations, the gifts—was done on a large scale. She had to have the largest tree, the biggest spread of goodies, and the most presents under the tree of anyone I ever knew. She was an incredible lady."

"She still is."

"Yes, of course." *Tell him now, Becky. Tell him the truth before it's too late. Tell him!* She drew in a shuddering breath and cleared her throat. "Rand?" Her fingers clenched and her throat constricted.

He looked at her, a smile playing on his lips. "What is it, Becky? You have an odd expression on your face."

"It's about my grandmother. I wanted to tell you the other day, but—"

Rand glanced at his watch. "I'm not trying to put you off, Becky. I want to hear all about your grandmother. But if we don't get going and do our shopping, we won't have time to take a tree and gifts to my grandmother tonight."

She exhaled, her shoulders slumping with dismay and relief. "Maybe later tonight then?" she bleated. "It's important."

He reached for her hand. "I'm sure it is, Becky. Later, okay? After we've seen Grams?"

She nodded, wondering if she would be able to summon the courage later. Merely contemplating her confession had left her drained, her mind numb. As they headed to the mall, she stared out the car window at the brightly decorated houses and shops, her mind too preoccupied for genuine conversation.

Rand noticed her silence. "A penny for your thoughts."

She chuckled. "They're worth at least a nickel."

"Okay. I'll go as high as a dime."

"Sold."

"Well?"

She hedged. "Nothing special. My mind was just wandering. See? Not even worth a penny."

"I'll be the judge of that."

"I was just thinking how unpredictable life is. What are the chances that we would end up being friends, seeing each other like this?"

"Even more amazing, what are the chances our grandmothers would meet and become friends?"

Becky looked away. "Yes, amazing."

Rand pulled into the mall's sprawling parking area and found an empty space close to the entrance. "Think of it, Becky. If it weren't for your grandmother, you and I wouldn't have gotten acquainted. You were so quiet in class. We probably would have remained nothing more than teacher and pupil. But once I fell in love with your grandmother, I knew I'd be crazy about you too."

She managed a self-conscious chuckle. "Maybe it's really my grandmother you love."

"I think that would be stretching the idea of a May-December romance. Besides, you're very much like your grandmother, only younger and prettier."

In a small voice she murmured, "I hope you're not just seeing me through rose-colored glasses."

Rand turned off the engine, swiveled in his seat, and plucked off his wire-rim spectacles. "These lenses look clear to me. I think I'm seeing things pretty clearly." He tilted her chin up to his. "You look troubled, Becky. Something wrong?"

She drew back. "No, I'm fine. Just a lot on my mind."

He kissed her forehead, then turned and opened his door. "Come on. Let's go in the mall and catch a little Christmas spirit. You'll feel like a new woman!"

She opened her door and stepped out. Under her breath she muttered, "No thank you. Being two women is enough!"

During the next hour they visited four shops in the mall. Becky helped Rand pick out a robe, toiletries, candy, photo album, and silver picture frame for Myrtle. "You can put a nice picture of yourself in the frame," she suggested. "Myrtle will love it."

Rand squeezed her hand. "Maybe I'll put in a picture of the two of us. She'd like that even better."

"What a wonderful idea!" Then her mirth faded. "But we don't have a picture of the two of us."

"That's a situation we'll have to remedy." They walked on, passing a bookstore, video arcade, and card shop. Suddenly, Rand clasped Becky's arm and exclaimed, "Look, there's our answer."

She followed his gaze to a photo booth beside the food court.

"How about it, Becky? It'll give us four pictures for two dollars."

"Can't beat the price."

"Then let's go for it." Rand put in the money and pushed back the curtains. They both peered in, then looked at each other and broke into laughter. "Sorry, Becky. We're going to be a couple of sardines."

"What can we expect for the price? Glamour photos?"

Rand stepped back and made a little bow. "You first."

"No, I think you'd better get in first. It's going to be a tight squeeze."

He grinned. "Now that sounds promising."

She waited while he stepped into the cramped booth and sat down on the little stool. After a moment he got up and adjusted the stool. "Too high. It'll cut off the tops of our heads." Finally he settled back down, scooting as close as he could to the far side. "Your turn, Becky."

With a giggle she stepped inside and squeezed in beside Rand. He slipped his arm around her and pulled her close until his chin nuzzled her hair. His nearness made her light-headed.

"Can you breathe?" he asked.

"Barely." She wasn't about to explain that it was his delightful proximity that stole her breath away.

"Watch the birdie, Becky!"

"What birdie?"

"I don't know. That's what they always say."

"Stop clowning around, or we'll look like idiots."

"Who's clowning? This is my natural face."

The first picture flashed while they were still talking.

"I wasn't ready," she protested. "I had my mouth wide open."

He laughed. "Those are the breaks. I was looking cross-eyed."

"You were not!"

"Okay, I wasn't." He whisked off his glasses. "Now I'll look like an owl. I'm blind as a bat."

"Hush, or we'll miss the next flash."

They managed to smile for the second picture and both stuck out their tongues for the third. For the fourth, Rand clasped her face in his firm grip and kissed her soundly. They were still kissing when they realized the pictures were ready and someone else was waiting for the booth.

They clambered out with a mumbled apology to the next customer in line, retrieved their photo strip, and hurried away, stifling their laughter. When they were some distance away, they sat down on a cement bench and examined the pictures.

"Not too bad, Rand, considering we were making complete fools of ourselves."

"Are you kidding? I look like Sylvester the Cat!"

"You do not. Look at me! I look like a guppy with my mouth open so wide."

"You have a lovely mouth. It's just open a little wider than usual."

"Thanks a lot."

He winked. "What can I say, Becky? You bring out the mischief in me."

"I'll take that as a compliment."

"No, this is a compliment." He leaned over and whispered in her ear, "You're the most beautiful person I've ever met, and I adore you."

"Rand, I adore you too." She slipped her arm in his and laid her head on his shoulder, joy singing in her heart like a hundred violins. So this is what it felt like to be deliriously, rapturously in love!

After a minute Rand stood up and pulled Becky up beside him, the levity in his voice giving way to a more serious tone. "As much as I love sitting here with you, we'd better go shop for that tree and decorations and get over to the nursing home before Grams falls asleep."

At the mention of Myrtle and the nursing home, the evening suddenly seemed fraught with dark foreboding. Splinters of anxiety and guilt punctured Becky's euphoria while stark reality jarred her out of her fanciful reverie. As happy as she was right now, at any moment it could all come crashing down around her. Once Rand knew the truth, she could lose him forever.

eleven

Myrtle Watson's wrinkled face lit up when her grandson walked in brandishing an armload of gifts and a plucky little Christmas tree with shiny bulbs and gleaming garlands. Becky followed with more gifts, lingering a step behind, not wanting to steal Rand's thunder.

Myrtle's face had never looked more radiant. "Rand, Dear, you've made an old lady's dreams come true—to have one more Christmas with all the little treasures and trimmings of home!"

Rand motioned Becky over beside him. "Becky helped me, Grams, so you have her to thank for picking out the right gifts."

Becky flashed a wry smile. "Or to blame, as the case may be. If there's something you don't like we can exchange it for something you like."

"Oh, my darlings, I'm sure I'll love everything. You've made me very happy."

After Rand set the artificial tree on the table beside Myrtle's bed, Becky arranged the presents around it. Then Rand plugged in the tree, and they all gazed at the twinkling lights and sparkling ornaments.

Myrtle brushed at a tear. "Reminds me of Christmases from my childhood. But in those days we chopped down our own trees and made our own ornaments. We strung berries and popcorn and made stars out of tin foil and angels out of tissue paper."

"It sounds wonderful," said Becky.

Rand fluffed his grandmother's pillows and kissed her forehead. "How are you feeling today, Grams?"

"I'm fine, Dear. Especially now that you're here."

Becky waited for Myrtle to tell Rand about her bruises and the abuse she had suffered last night at the hands of a staff member. But she said nothing. Becky suppressed the impulse to bring up the subject. It was the elderly Rebecca Sterling Myrtle had confided in, not the young Becky Chandler. Still, Rand needed to know the truth. Once Becky shed her disguise, she would no longer be able to frequent the halls of Morning Glory unnoticed. It would be up to Rand to see that his grandmother received proper care.

Becky watched as Rand smoothed Myrtle's gnarled hand with gentle fingers. "Grams, I hear Becky's grandmother visited you this morning."

Becky watched Myrtle's expression for any evidence of doubt or suspicion. *Does she know I'm really Rebecca Sterling? Or does she think, like Rand, that we're two different people?*

"Yes, Rand, we had a very nice visit. She's a dear friend."

Becky expelled a sigh of relief. Myrtle wasn't suspicious. For the moment she was still in the clear.

Rand showed his grandmother the photos they had taken at the mall. She smiled as she examined each one, then turned her old eyes up to Becky. "You make a nice couple, Dear. It's time for my grandson to think about marriage. I have prayed for a wife for him for a long time. Before I die, I want to know he has someone to love him unconditionally. The right woman. A godly woman. Perhaps it is you."

Becky's face grew warm. She lowered her lashes, scouring her mind for a coherent reply. "I. . .I don't know the answer to that, Mrs. Watson. But I do know Rand is blessed to have such a caring grandmother."

Myrtle winked at her grandson. "Rand, I think she's a keeper."

His warm gaze met Becky's. "I think you may be right, Grams." He reached for Becky's hand. "But before the two of us embarrass her to death, I think we'd better go and let you get some sleep."

Myrtle's eyes grew moist as Rand kissed her good-bye. "I will have pleasant dreams tonight, Dear, thanks to you."

"I'm glad. I'll stop by tomorrow, Grams, after my classes."

Myrtle pulled him closer and whispered, "Rand, don't let your lovely lady get away."

He chuckled. "Don't worry, Grams. I may not be the smartest man in the world, but I'm no fool."

When Becky kissed Myrtle good night, the elderly woman closed her eyes and murmured serenely, "So like your grandmother."

"Thank you." Becky tucked the covers around Myrtle and turned off the light. "You know my grandmother would do anything to make sure you're okay."

"I know."

Becky set her handbag at the foot of the bed, then turned and followed Rand out the door. They were halfway to the lobby when she said, "Rand, I left my purse on the bed. I'll be right back."

"I'll go back for it."

"No, please, I know right where it is. You go on and I'll catch up with you."

"If you're sure."

"Positive." She turned and hurried back down the hall before Rand changed his mind and followed her. She slipped into Myrtle's room and, with quiet, deliberate motions, she picked up the nearest chair and carried it over to the console holding the television set. Gingerly she stepped up on the chair, felt for the camcorder, then turned it on and pressed the Record button. Would it even show anything in such low light conditions? A night-light was on by the bed, and faint rays of light streamed in from the hallway, but most of the room was in shadows. *This is probably an exercise in futility, but I've got to give it one more chance.* She stepped down, carried the chair back to its usual position, and seized her purse from the bed.

Myrtle stirred. "Rebecca, is that you?"

"Yes, Dear. Sleep well."

"You too, dear friend."

By the time Becky joined Rand in the lobby, her heart was pounding and her mouth was too dry to speak. Did Rand suspect she had ulterior motives for going back?

He smiled. "I see you found it."

"Yes. It was right where I left it."

As they walked out to his car, her pulse relaxed and she began to feel calm again. All had gone well. She would return in the morning for the camcorder, and there would likely be nothing of consequence on it. But at least she had gone the extra mile. Whether she had enough evidence or not, she would have a good talk with the management of Morning Glory. They needed to know one or more staff members were mistreating the residents.

At Rand's car, Becky waited for him to open the door. The night air was fresh, brisk, and invigorating. She loved California in December. While the rest of the country was bringing out snowplows, Californians could still enjoy sunshine and a temperate climate. And a perfect, balmy evening with someone they loved.

"Are you ready to go, Becky?"

She looked up, startled, and realized Rand was waiting for her to get in the car. "I'm sorry. I was just enjoying the lovely evening."

"No problem. It is nice. Not too warm, not too cold."

Settling into the passenger seat, she reminded herself the night wasn't over. Perhaps it was just beginning. Would she find the courage to tell Rand the truth? And would he hate her for deceiving him? A shiver went through her. Was this the beginning of the end?

The drive to her apartment took just a few minutes. That didn't give Becky much time to delve into such a serious subject. She considered inviting Rand up to her apartment to talk, but that didn't seem wise either. Someone seeing them might get the wrong idea. She could suggest they stop somewhere for coffee, but she didn't want a crowd around when she launched into such a sensitive topic. *Lord, help me! I'm feeling so weak. I need Your strength. Help me to tell Rand the truth tonight!*

It seemed less than two minutes had passed when he pulled into the parking lot at her apartment and turned off the engine. He shifted in his seat, facing her. In the shadows his handsome face looked solemn. "Becky, we need to talk."

She twisted her purse strap. "I know, Rand. I've been waiting for this."

"You have?"

"I told you earlier I have something to tell you."

He scratched his head. "You mean, about your grandmother?"

"About my grandmother and me, and a lot of other things."

Rand took her hand and brought it to his lips. "You know I want to hear anything you have to say, but tonight I just want to talk about us."

"Us?" She smiled. "I like the way you say that."

"So do I, Becky. Grams isn't the only one who's been praying for me to find the right girl. It's been a prayer of mine for years. At one time I thought that girl might be Gloria, but I know now she's not the one for me."

"Because she's not a Christian."

"It's more than that, Becky. I want a woman who will share my faith in every way. Someone I can pray with and share my struggles with. Someone who wants a close walk with Christ the same as I do."

She nodded. "I admire you for your strong faith."

"That's just it, Becky. I'm not strong. The more I know of Jesus, the more I realize how far I have to go in my relationship with Him. I know what I need to do to maintain close fellowship, and yet so often I choose the easier way. I don't nurture my relationship with Him the way I should."

"None of us do, Rand. We all fall so far short of pleasing Him. It's a daily struggle to choose Him instead of ourselves."

"Exactly. And you understand that. You know where I'm coming from."

"Yes, I'm guilty too." *Guilty of so much more than you, Rand!*

"What I want in a wife is someone to hold me accountable, someone I can share the spiritual side of my life with. Someone I can pray with, whose first priority will be raising our children to love the Lord."

She chuckled. "Children? Aren't you rushing it a bit?"

He pressed her hand against his cheek. "Not at all, Becky. I'm responsible for my children's spiritual lives. The best thing I can do for them is to give them a mother who loves and serves the Lord."

She squirmed in her seat, wondering if she could handle the direction this conversation was going. "You really do think ahead, Rand."

"You do want children, don't you, Becky?"

She met his gaze. His face was shadowed, except where rays from the streetlight caught the twinkle in his dusky blue eyes. "Of course I want children. A baker's dozen. Actually, not that many. Maybe two or three."

He kissed her palm. "That's a good start."

"What are you saying, Rand?" *Please don't be proposing. It'll just make what I have to tell you that much harder!*

"I'm not sure what I'm saying, Becky. Except that I believe God brought us together for a reason. You're a woman of strong faith. You have a wonderful heritage in your grandmother. I can see you becoming just like her."

Becky winced. "So can I. More than you know!"

"And that's the kind of person I want to marry. Someone

who walks with God faithfully through her entire lifetime."

Becky withdrew her hand. An ache was forming in her chest. "I'm not my grandmother, Rand. I mean, I am my grandmother, but I'm not. Oh, I don't know what I mean!"

Rand slipped his arm around her and drew her close. "It's okay, Becky. I can see I'm coming on too strong. I just wanted to give you some things to think about."

She blinked back tears of frustration. He was saying everything she wanted to hear, but surely he would take it all back when she told him her secret. "Don't worry, Rand. I have plenty to think about."

He tilted her face up to his. "Here's the main thing to think about, Becky." He kissed her with a tenderness that made her melt inside, then whispered, "I think I'm falling in love with you."

twelve

I think I'm falling in love with you.

Those were the first words that came to Becky's mind when she woke the next morning. She rolled over in bed and gazed up at the ceiling, replaying the memories of last night, of Rand confessing how he felt about her. Those were the words she had always dreamed of hearing from the man she loved.

But she had resisted telling him she felt the same way, partly out of guilt and fear. He only thought he knew her. Would he still proclaim his love if he knew she had made a mockery of his trust by pretending to be someone she wasn't? He practically admitted he loved her because she was so much like her beloved, highly venerated grandmother—a woman who didn't exist. Actually, she had existed, but the real Rebecca Sterling, her own precious grandmother, had died nearly ten years ago. Becky's portrayal was a poor imitation. She would never be the woman her dear grandmother had been.

Still, portraying Rebecca Sterling had changed Becky in significant ways. She would always be a kinder, gentler, more loving person for having known and walked in Rebecca Sterling's footsteps. But was that enough to convince Rand that Rebecca Chandler was the one for him? Or would the magnitude of her deception outweigh whatever good she had accomplished?

She hadn't told him the truth last night because it seemed somehow inappropriate to break their romantic mood with a confession. Or maybe she had just chickened out again. Whatever it was, she would not fail today. She was determined to tell him everything.

113

To prove her resolve, she climbed out of bed, grabbed the phone, and dialed Rand's home phone number. She gave a sigh of disappointment when his answering machine came on. She refused to confess like this, but at least she would let him know her intentions. She forced her voice to sound positive and confident. "Rand, this is Becky. Last night was wonderful! But I didn't tell you what I've been trying to tell you for weeks now. I have a confession to make, and I just pray you'll understand when I explain everything. So please call me and let me know when we can get together to talk. Thanks. I'll see you soon."

There! She had done it. Or nearly done it. At least Rand would know she had something important to reveal.

The next item on her agenda was to put out the bags of clothes, wigs, and makeup for the Good Will pickup. She pulled on her robe, then gathered the two large paper sacks in her arms and carried them outside. She propped them beside her door where they would be easily seen from the street. She gave the contents a final, lingering glance—the apparel and accoutrements of the old Rebecca—then slipped back inside and closed the door. It was done! She had kept back just enough items for one last appearance at Morning Glory.

"Good-bye, Rebecca Sterling," she whispered, fighting tears. "I'll miss you, but I'll never forget you. You changed my life forever."

But there was no time for sentimentality this morning. She had to shower, don her disguise, and head over to Morning Glory, where she would retrieve her camcorder and say goodbye to Myrtle. Then she would find Rand and tell him the whole complicated story of her masquerade. She would share with him whatever evidence she had compiled of abuse at the nursing home, and together they would decide what steps to take to ensure the safety of Myrtle and the other residents.

As she showered, dressed, and applied her latex mask, she

mused that everything seemed so clear to her this morning. She knew exactly what she had to do to complete her work as the elderly Rebecca. By this evening her whole quixotic venture into old age would be behind her, Rand would know the truth, and, God willing, they would begin to build their life together, based on honesty and trust.

The Scripture came to her, *You shall know the truth, and the truth shall make you free.* Those words took on new meaning for her today. She would indeed feel free once the truth was out and she no longer had to pretend to be two people. Only now, with the end in sight, did she realize what a heavy toll her masquerade had taken on her. The thought struck as an epiphany of sorts. Deceiving the people she loved had cost her peace of mind and joy in her faith. How long had it been since she had genuinely experienced God's closeness? The weight of guilt and anxiety over her deception had sapped her spiritual energy and diverted her attention from Christ.

As Becky placed her silver-gray wig on her head, she said aloud, "I didn't realize what was happening, Lord. I didn't notice how far we were drifting apart. I'm sorry. Help me to do the right thing and get close to You again. Forgive me for getting so caught up in my own problems that I turned my eyes from You. Help me to give back to You all the things I'm clutching too tightly in my hands. I just want to please You, Father." Almost as an afterthought, she added, "And please be with me this one last time as I go to Morning Glory as the old Rebecca. Let me get the proof of abuse and neglect I need to make positive changes for the dear people there."

She felt a bittersweet sensation, almost like nostalgia, as she wrapped elastic bandages around her padded legs and tied her orthopedic shoes. She adjusted her pillbox hat and patted her wispy gray hair into place. Finally, pulling on her white gloves, she studied her reflection in the floor-length mirror. It was amazing how thoroughly she became another person once she was in disguise. Her whole mind and thought processes changed; her outlook and attitude shifted; she felt different; she looked at the world differently. Once in costume, she moved and reacted as an elderly woman and expected to be treated like one. She wouldn't experience this sensation again for another fifty years!

It was after nine o'clock when Rebecca arrived at the nursing home. As she shuffled down the long corridor, she realized she would never pass through these halls again as an old woman. Her senses seemed jarringly acute today. She was aware of rank smells permeating the air, blending with the pungency of disinfectant. A low moan emanated from one room; at the end of the hall a withered woman in a wheelchair chattered loudly to no one in particular. A television set droned in another room. She noticed Dirk, the attendant with the glaring eyes, leave one room and cross the hall to another. Selena, the bright young nurse Rebecca had met during a recent visit, was carrying on an animated conversation with an orderly.

When Rebecca arrived at Myrtle's room, she was surprised to see the door shut. Usually it was open at least a crack. Myrtle liked feeling she was in touch with the rest of the world, not shut away alone.

Knocking briskly, Rebecca waited a moment, then turned the knob and pushed the door open slowly. She didn't want to startle Myrtle or interrupt some nursing home routine. When she stepped inside, her eyes went directly to Myrtle's bed. It was empty. The mattress, stripped of sheets and blankets, looked stark, ominous. . .solitary. An icy, shuddering sense of dread clutched Rebecca's heart.

Myrtle's dead!

Rebecca dropped her cane and scrambled across the tile floor in her geriatric shoes to the bathroom. It was empty. Aloud she cried, "Where did she go? Where could they have taken her?"

Panic electrified every nerve ending as she grabbed her cane and hurried out into the corridor, looking for answers. She shambled down the hall to Selena and gripped her arm. "Where's Myrtle?" she croaked.

For a moment the young nurse looked puzzled, perhaps wondering how a decrepit old lady could demonstrate such strength and determination. "Oh, Myrtle Watson? They took her to the hospital."

Rebecca almost forgot her antiquated voice. "What happened? Is she okay?"

"She fell while going to the bathroom. We had to call an ambulance and have her taken to the hospital. She may have broken her hip."

"Does her grandson know?"

"I'm sure they called him. It happened sometime in the night."

"Was she alone?"

"Yes, I believe she was."

"Who found her?"

The nurse gave Rebecca a curious frown. "One of our attendants."

Rebecca held her impatience at bay. "Which one?"

"I think it was Dirk. Dirk Seuer."

A chill seized Rebecca. Dirk, the evil-eyed bruiser! She didn't trust that man. There was something cruel and unfeeling about him. She couldn't prove it, but she knew he had abused Myrtle in the past. Rebecca could only imagine what might have happened last night.

The camera! I turned it on before I left. Maybe it shows the sequence of events.

Rebecca thanked Selena for her information, then turned and scuffled back to Myrtle's room. Once inside, she quietly closed the door, pushed the chair over to the wall holding the television set, climbed up, and dislodged the camcorder from the console. Just as she stepped back down, the door opened. Her eyes flew to the strapping figure in the doorway.

Dirk!

With a swift, instinctive gesture Rebecca stuffed the camcorder into her roomy handbag and reached for her cane on the bed. Dirk strode across the room and grabbed for the purse. She swung it out of his grasp.

"What you got in there, old woman?"

"Nothing for you, young man!" Hunching over and tapping her cane briskly on the floor, she tried maneuvering around him, her eyes fixed on the half-open door.

Dirk stepped squarely in front of her, his beefy hands on his hips. "You ain't going nowhere 'til you give me that purse."

She took a step backward. "You let me out of here or I'll scream."

He stepped forward, towering over her. "Go ahead. They'll just think you're one of the loonies in this place."

Rebecca's heart throbbed in her throat. Her face felt prickly and flushed under the latex mask. Did Dirk suspect who she was? "I just came to see my friend, Myrtle," she bleated.

"Too bad. She ain't here. Now tell me what you got in that bag. A camera?"

"None of your business!" Rebecca made another attempt for the door, but Dirk caught her by the arm. She twisted out of his grasp and nearly reached the door when he seized her handbag with his big paw. Steeling herself, she jerked hard on the strap, wrenching the purse free from his grasp.

Dirk stared down at his empty hands, then glared at Rebecca. "Where'd an old lady like you get all that strength?"

"I work out!" She darted around him and was nearly out the door when his fingers clenched the back of her shawl. Stumbling backward, she waved her cane until it hit its mark with a solid thump. Dirk made a gasping sound but still held tight to her shawl. With a zigzag motion, she freed herself and ran out of the room, slamming the door behind her.

For a split second she looked up and down the hall, empty now except for the dithering lady in her wheelchair. Clutching her handbag to her chest, Rebecca turned left and strode toward the lobby as fast as her flowing skirts and geriatric shoes would allow. Her heart hammered as she heard a door slam, then footsteps echoing on the tile floor behind her. Glancing back, she saw Dirk gaining on her, holding his bleeding forehead. He sidestepped the old woman in the wheelchair and lunged for her.

Throwing her cane behind her, she picked up her skirts and began to run. She glanced back over her shoulder in time to see Dirk stumble over the clattering cane, his husky arms flailing the air. Looking forward again, she spotted an orderly heading her way, sporting an enormous bag of laundry. This was a collision waiting to happen.

"Stop that crazy woman!" Dirk shouted. "She attacked me!"

After a moment of bewilderment, the orderly got the message and stepped in front of Rebecca, blocking her access to the lobby. She looked back in desperation. Dirk was just behind her now, still holding his injured head, his face crimson with rage. He was so close, she could feel his hot breath on her.

She was trapped.

Reacting out of pure survivor's instinct, she darted around the orderly and shoved him at Dirk. As she bolted down a side hall, she caught a glimpse of the pandemonium she'd left behind—Dirk colliding with the orderly and bouncing off the overstuffed laundry bag, then the two of them tumbling to the floor in a sprawling heap.

But she wasn't safe yet. It would take the two men only seconds to catch up with her again. Where could she hide? She didn't dare risk harm to any of the residents by entering their rooms. Then she saw her answer. The ladies' rest room! After glancing up and down the hall to make sure no one was watching, she slipped inside. She entered the farthest stall, locked it, sat down, put her feet up, circled her knees with her arms, and pressed her face into the folds of her skirt to muffle her heavy breathing.

Please don't let them find me here, please!

After a moment she heard male voices in the hall outside the rest room. They sounded angry, agitated. One voice was Dirk's. She could hardly hear what he was saying over the fierce pounding of her heart. Something like, "Crazy woman. . . find her. . .don't let her get away. . .she can't go far!"

Rebecca heard the bathroom door creak open and held her breath. Then silence. She closed her eyes, waiting for the click of footsteps on the ceramic tile.

Then, to her amazement, the door closed and she heard the men's muffled voices receding, growing faint. They were gone. It was quiet again.

Thank You, Lord! Thank You, thank You, thank You!

She scrambled out of the stall and sprang into action, yanking off her wig, pillbox hat, and gloves, then stripping the latex from her face, even though it stung and left red welts on her skin. She pulled off her bulky sweater and pleated skirt, then peeled off her bulky bodysuit and support hose. Her breath was coming in short gasps as she unwound the stretchy bandages from her legs.

When she had sloughed off all of her old-age accoutrements and apparel, she gathered everything up in her arms and stuffed it into the trash can. Fortunately she had worn a tank top and black stretch leggings under her costume.

She fished in her handbag for her hairbrush and cosmetics. With trembling fingers she applied foundation, blush, eyeliner, and lipstick, then brushed her hair vigorously until it fluffed nicely around her face. She paused, catching her breath, and studied herself in the mirror. Considering the speed of her makeover, she had accomplished quite a transformation. A young, shapely, attractive woman gazed back at her.

Now to see if she could escape without arousing anyone's suspicions. She opened the door a crack and peeked out. No one in sight. She slung her purse over her shoulder and stepped into the hallway. With her chin high and her back straight, she strode down the corridor toward the lobby. But first she had to pass the hall leading to Myrtle's room.

She cast a sidelong glance to her left, then her right. A nurse was chatting with a resident but neither looked her way. She quickened her pace. The hall seemed to stretch on forever. Then, just as she entered the lobby, she spotted Dirk and the orderly conversing near the information desk. Their expressions were solemn and Dirk held a compress against his bleeding forehead. She had to pass right by them to get out the door. She straightened her shoulders and kept walking, but she was shaking so hard she wondered if her legs would carry her.

"Yea, though I walk through the valley of the shadow. . .I will fear no evil. . ." Keeping her head high and her eyes straight ahead, she took long, limber strides across the foyer. The two men had stopped talking, and she sensed their curious gazes on her. Did they recognize her? Suspect something? Perhaps Dirk recognized the purse she was carrying. Or her shoes. She hadn't been able to change her shoes. What young woman wore shoes like this?

One of the men whistled.

That's a good sign. It shows they're not thinking about finding an old lady anymore!

"Hey, Girlie, you're gonna freeze in that skimpy getup!"

Dirk's voice.

She kept walking, pretending she hadn't heard.

With a slow, measured pace she pushed open the glass

double doors of Morning Glory and stepped out into the cold, bright December day. Once outside, she broke into a run for her car, the chill air filling her lungs. She heaved a sigh of relief when she was safely behind the wheel with the doors locked.

She drove straight to the hospital to see Myrtle Watson but couldn't bring herself to go inside until she stopped trembling. What was wrong with her? The nightmare was over. She was safe. But it would take awhile for her body to catch up. She sat in her car in the parking lot for nearly a half hour, waiting for her heart rate to return to normal and the terror in her chest to subside.

Finally, when she felt almost normal again, she got out and scrounged around in her trunk for her denim jacket and a better pair of shoes. Fortunately she kept a spare pair of sneakers handy for just such occasions as this! Well, actually, she had never had an occasion like this, and she prayed she never would again.

The craziness was over. She was done once and for all with her elderly persona. Rebecca Sterling was a thing of the past. Dead. Kaput! Finished. If Becky hadn't been certain before, there was no question now. Never again for the rest of her life would she subject herself to the weirdness and unpredictability of portraying someone she wasn't, no matter how noble the cause.

And now it was time to pick up the pieces of her life unencumbered by her alter ego. She was free. She was nobody else on earth but the young Rebecca Sterling Chandler. The sensation was invigorating.

With a fresh burst of resolve, she marched into the hospital in her denim jacket, sneakers, and stretch leggings, her skin smarting from the latex but her youthful face greeting the world.

But once inside the sprawling vestibule with its white,

antiseptic walls and impersonal corridors shooting off in every direction, new concerns shadowed her thoughts.

How is Myrtle? Did she break her hip? Did they take her to surgery? Will she survive? Is Rand with her, sitting by her bedside, needing someone to comfort him? *How will I find the right words when I don't even know if Myrtle is dead or alive? Heavenly Father, what pain and heartaches will I encounter in Myrtle's room? And will I be wise and strong enough to help these two people I love so dearly?*

thirteen

When Becky stopped at the information desk and inquired about Myrtle Watson, the disinterested receptionist checked her records and replied blandly, "We don't show a room for her yet. When was she admitted?"

Becky clutched the edge of the desk. "I don't know. Sometime in the night. You must have some information."

"I'm sorry, Miss."

"Please check again. I've got to see her."

"There's nothing more I can tell you. They're probably still doing tests and assessing her condition. You might want to check back later."

Becky could feel her agitation growing. "Her grandson—Rand Cameron—must be here. Do you know where I can find him?"

"You might check the waiting room. It's down the hall, to the left."

"Thank you." Becky nearly ran the length of the hall. Breathless, she entered the waiting room, her eyes moving past the green vinyl couches and utilitarian furniture to the single occupant—a tall, raven-haired man staring out the window. "Rand!"

He turned and met her gaze, but before he could speak she crossed the room and went into his arms. He hugged her so hard she winced.

"Honey, I was praying you'd come. I kept phoning your apartment. Where have you been?"

"It doesn't matter. I'll explain later. How's your grandmother?"

"I don't know." He led her over to the nearest couch and

they sat down. He swiveled, facing her, and ran his fingers through the tousled curls beside her temple. "They haven't told me a thing."

"You haven't seen her?"

"Just for a few minutes in the emergency room. She looked bad, Becky. She was in pain and seemed so confused. I've never seen her like that."

"Rand, I'm so sorry." Becky drew in a deep breath. Was this the appropriate time to tell Rand the truth? "Actually, I went to the nursing home this morning to visit your grandmother."

"Oh, that's where you were! Thank you for thinking of her."

"You know how much I care about her."

"I know. You and your grandmother are devoted to Grams. That's why I kept phoning you. No one answered, so evidently you were already at the nursing home."

"Her room was empty when I got there. The nurse said she had fallen in the night and might have broken her hip."

Rand's expression darkened. "Yes, she fell, but we don't know yet about her hip. They took her to X-ray and they're running tests. We should hear something anytime now."

Becky ran her fingertips over the back of his hand. "This has to be so hard for you, Rand. I know how much you love your grandmother."

He smiled and pulled her against him, draping his arm over her shoulder. "Grams has been like a mother to me. I don't know what I would do without her."

"I'm praying she'll be okay."

"Me too." They were silent for a moment, then Rand nuzzled her hair with his chin. "I can't tell you how good it is to have you here with me, Becky. It makes all the difference in the world. A few minutes ago I was feeling so blue and alone, but just holding you in my arms makes me feel like everything is going to be okay."

She nestled closer to his chest. "I love being in your arms."

"I'm glad, because I plan never to let you go."

"That's fine with me." How was it possible an hour ago her very life was in danger and now she felt so wonderfully safe and at home?

He tilted her chin up and searched her eyes. "Did that just sound like a proposal and an acceptance?"

A tickle of delight somersaulted inside her. "I don't know. What kind of proposal did you have in mind?"

He chuckled. "This isn't the right time or place for a marriage proposal. But I do propose we keep that possibility in mind for discussion in the near future, when the time and place are right."

She stifled a laugh. "That's a convoluted answer, if I ever heard one. But, strange as it seems, I understood every word."

"That means our minds are in sync or we're both crazy."

"Crazy? Never!" She traced the smattering of fine dark hairs on his wrist. "I like to think we're totally in sync about everything, Rand—which reminds me. I really do need to talk to you about my grandmother."

He glanced around. "Yes, where is the darling old dowager? I want her here. She's the only person I know who can cheer up Grams in these awful circumstances. In fact, I thought she might have come with you now, if you were both at the nursing home."

"No, it wasn't both of us. Not exactly."

"I'm confused. She was either there or she wasn't."

"That's what I want to explain, Rand." *Lord, help me find the courage to tell him the truth!*

"No need to explain, Becky. If she didn't go with you to the nursing home, she must still be at your apartment. So, don't worry, I've got it covered."

She studied him, perplexed. "You've got what covered?"

"Getting your grandmother here to the hospital."

Becky's heart caught in her throat. "Rand, what did you do?"

He gave her a puzzled glance. "There's nothing to worry about, Becky. When no one answered your phone, I figured you were out, but your grandmother was there and just didn't hear the ring. So I phoned Gloria and asked if she'd go over and pick up your grandmother and bring her to the hospital."

Becky stared at Rand in astonishment. "You called Gloria?"

"Sure. Why not? We're still friends."

"You mean you asked Gloria Farrington to bring my grandmother here?"

"What's the problem, Becky? I was beside myself. I couldn't reach you, and I couldn't think of anyone else to call."

A sour taste rose in Becky's throat. "You shouldn't have done that, Rand."

"Why not?"

"Because Gloria can't bring my grandmother to the hospital."

"Why? She's not ill, is she?"

Becky's stomach churned. This wasn't going the way she had planned. "No, that's not it."

Rand was beginning to sound impatient. "Then just tell me what's going on, Becky. Where is your grandmother? Where is Rebecca Sterling?"

Before Becky could reply, a feminine voice trumpeted, "She's right here!"

They both turned toward the shapely woman who came flouncing through the waiting room doorway. Gloria Farrington, looking smug and triumphant, stood holding two bulky paper sacks in her arms.

Becky froze. *No, it can't be! Not my Good Will donations!*

Gloria sashayed over to Rand, yanked a gray wig out of one sack, and waved it before his eyes. "Here, Rand, Darling. You wanted Rebecca Sterling? You've got her!" She dropped the wig on his lap, then pulled a shawl and pillbox hat from the other bag and dropped them into his hands.

He stared at the items as if they might burn his palms. "What is this?"

With a brittle smile Gloria continued to empty out the bags, dropping one item after another on Rand's lap, on the table, on the floor—elastic bandages, support hose and shoes, jewelry and white gloves, sweaters, dresses, and undergarments.

Rand stared at the paraphernalia in openmouthed bewilderment. "What's going on?"

Gloria pointed a shiny red fingernail at Becky. "Why don't you ask your innocent little girlfriend?"

Rand looked at her, his skin blanched white, his brow furrowed. "What is this stuff, Becky?"

She sank back against the couch, her extremities numb, her mind short-circuited with shame, her tongue cleaving to the roof of her mouth. She had no excuse. No defense. She was guilty of the worst possible deception, and now Rand was hearing the terrible truth from someone else—a cruel, ruthless woman who hated Becky for stealing her man.

Unlike Becky, Gloria Farrington wasn't at a loss for words. She spewed her venom in a streaming diatribe of accusations. "Don't you get it, Rand? This girl who pretends to be such a goody-goody Christian has been lying to you from the beginning. There is no such person as Rebecca Sterling. Becky has been dressing up like an old lady. She's been playing a part, deceiving you and your grandmother. She made a fool of all of us!"

Rand's eyes silently begged for an explanation. "Is it true, Becky? Rebecca Sterling doesn't exist?"

Becky finally found her voice, but the words came out in a broken whisper. "She. . .existed. She was. . .my grandmother."

"You mean, she is your grandmother. She does exist."

A tear trickled down Becky's cheek. "She died ten years ago."

Something significant shifted in Rand's expression. The

bewilderment yielded to doubt and suspicion. His eyes narrowed and his mouth hardened. "Then you're saying she doesn't exist? You just pretended to be her?"

Gloria emptied out the remaining items and tossed the empty sacks on the floor. "It was more than a simple little pretense, Rand. Look at this stuff. This was a cold, calculating, well-executed hoax. She went to a lot of trouble to make people believe she was an old woman."

Rand lifted the silvery wig off his lap and dropped it on the table as if it were an animal that might bite. "So it's true, Becky? It was you all along? The woman we knew as your grandmother. . .was you?"

Becky was weeping now. "I'm sorry, Rand. I never meant to deceive you."

He stared at her as if she were a stranger, worse than a stranger. "I can't believe this, Becky. I can't take this all in. It makes no sense."

Gloria stood over him with her hands on her hips. "Of course it makes sense, Rand. She used her grandmother and your grandmother to finagle a relationship with you. She was just a mousy little girl in your class, one of hundreds of students, until you got acquainted with the elderly Rebecca Sterling. She must have known you were a sucker for old people. And what better way to win your heart than by exploiting your love for your grandmother!"

Becky seized Rand's arm. "It's not true. I love your grandmother! I would never do anything to hurt her—or you!"

Rand moved away from her touch. The shadow of doubt in his eyes gave way to seething anger. "But it appears you did do something to hurt us. You made us care about someone who. . .who wasn't even real!" He raked his fingers through his thick, ebony hair. "I can't believe it. When I think of all the times I took your grandmother into my confidence, all the times we chatted together like intimate friends! The things I told her that I thought were just between the two of us! And all the time it was you, Becky? You in disguise? I was telling you all those things, and you never gave me the slightest hint it was you! That's beyond my comprehension! Why would you do something so outrageous, so contemptible?"

Becky choked back a sob. "I wanted to tell you, Rand. I tried so many times, but I couldn't find the words."

"You couldn't find the words to tell me the truth?" Rand stood up and paced the floor, shaking his head. "How you must have been laughing at me behind your back."

"I never laughed. Never!"

"Becky, Becky, how could you do this to me? You managed to play this bizarre little game flawlessly. You knew your lines. You never missed a beat. You deserve an Academy Award."

"Are you kidding, Rand? She deserves a jail cell!" Gloria wound her arm possessively around Rand's. "Darling, she ought to be arrested. She's an impostor. There must be a law against impersonating someone else. It's dishonest. It's fraud!"

Rand disengaged her arm from his. "Stop it, Gloria. I can't think straight."

"I'm just trying to help, Darling."

He strode across the room. "Leave me alone, both of you. I've got to sort this out."

Becky stood up, her ankles shaking. She was trembling from head to toe. "Rand, do you want me to leave?"

"Of course he does!" Gloria patted her blond bouffant hair, her steel-gray eyes drilling into Becky. "Haven't you humiliated him enough?"

Becky stared Gloria down. "I asked Rand, not you."

"Tell her, Rand. Make her go. She's a liar and a cheat."

Becky brushed at her tears. "I'll go, Rand, if that's what you want."

He stared at her, his eyes brimming with pain and disbelief. She winced. How could she have brought such misery to a man she loved so much?

He approached, circling her, raking his fingers through his mussed hair. "You just laid this bombshell on me, Becky, and now you want to go? What am I supposed to do with this incredible information?"

She shook her head, lowering her lashes. "I don't know."

"It changes everything, Becky. The way I see you. The way I see us. You must realize that. I don't know what we were to each other. What was that thing we shared—you and I? Love? Trust? A godly relationship? It couldn't have been any of those things, because we were living a lie!"

Her tears started again. She fished in her purse for a tissue and blew her nose. "You're right, Rand. I deceived you. I'm sorry. I'd better go."

His fingers grazed her arm, an electrifying touch. She hesitated, her pulse caught in mid beat. His eyes searched hers with a raw intensity that left her reeling. His voice emerged full of misery and yearning. "I thought I knew you, Becky. I thought we had something rare and wonderful."

She stretched out her hand, as if to caress his face. "We did, Rand. We do."

Jerking his head away, he turned his back to her. "Go home, Becky. We have nothing. It was all a sham, a farce. . .a terrible joke. Whatever it was, it's over."

A heavy silence settled over the room. Hugging her purse to her chest, Becky took several awkward steps toward the door, then glanced back sorrowfully at Rand. "I'm sorry. I hope someday you'll let me explain."

Gloria's abrasive voice broke in. "He doesn't want to hear your sorry excuses!"

Rand wheeled around and pointed an accusing finger at Gloria. "Shut up! You've said enough!"

With a faltering step backward, Gloria sniveled, "Don't bite my head off, Darling. I was just trying to help."

"I don't need your—"

"Professor Cameron?" a deep, rumbling voice called from the doorway.

They all turned to face the tall, bearded man in the crisp, white physician's coat. An eternity seemed to pass before the doctor announced solemnly, "I have news about your grandmother, Myrtle Watson."

fourteen

The bearded physician extended his hand to Rand. "I'm Dr. Castillo. I just left your grandmother."

Rand shook his hand. "How is she, Doctor?"

"Let's sit down a moment and talk."

Rand introduced Becky and Gloria to Dr. Castillo, then the four of them sat down. Becky wasn't sure she was welcome, but she joined them anyway, desperate to know how Myrtle was doing.

Dr. Castillo, a ruddy, sharp-featured man with shiny black hair, sat forward, tented his fingers, and cleared his throat. "The X-rays show that Myrtle did not break her hip."

Rand emitted a whistling sigh. "Thank God!"

Becky nodded. "Yes, thank God."

"But she did sustain some minor injuries, she's a little agitated, and her electrolytes seem a bit off. So we'd like to keep her here a day or two for observation."

"But she's going to be okay?" persisted Rand.

"I don't see why not. She's a strong woman for her age." Dr. Castillo paused, his shaggy brows furrowing in a scowl. "However, there is something I'm concerned about. She shows some bruising inconsistent with a fall."

Alarm edged Rand's voice. "What does that mean?"

"Perhaps nothing. Or perhaps your grandmother has been subjected to some sort of mistreatment."

Rand kneaded his hands, his forehead corrugated with misgivings. "I had hoped I was wrong, Doctor, but I think she may have been manhandled by some of the staff at the nursing home. I have no proof. It's only a suspicion. But I've had concerns about that place for some time now."

Becky opened her mouth to speak, to tell what she knew, then thought better of the idea. *I may have proof of abuse, Rand, but this isn't the time to discuss it. Idle speculation won't help Myrtle. First, I've got to make sure I have enough evidence to bring real changes at Morning Glory.*

Dr. Castillo stood up. "Professor, you may want to have a good heart-to-heart conversation with your grandmother about the treatment she's received. Some elderly people are afraid to say anything, afraid to make waves. They think people won't believe them or they'll be punished for their complaints."

Rand stood up too. "I'll talk to her, Doctor."

"Not today or tomorrow. Let her rest. I don't want anyone or anything upsetting her for the next twenty-four hours."

"Don't worry. I'll do all I can to keep her calm. When can I see her?"

"You can see her now. She's been taken to room 134. And, for the record, she's been asking for her grandson and her friend Rebecca."

Rand cast a dubious sidelong glance at Becky. "Her friend Rebecca? I don't know if that's possible."

"Do what you can, Professor. She needs all the support she can get."

"Thank you, Doctor." Rand shook his hand and Dr. Castillo strode away.

"What about it, Becky?" Rand's voice was thick with sarcasm, his gaze smoldering. "Do you want to do one last performance for my grandmother's sake?"

"I'll visit your grandmother, if that's what you're asking. But I won't go in disguise."

"Isn't it a little late to take the high moral road?" snapped Gloria. She held up the gray wig. "Here, go to it. After all, you've played the part lots of times before."

"Gloria has a point," said Rand, handing her the wig. "Grams wants to see Rebecca Sterling, not Becky Chandler."

Becky tossed the wig back in the sack. "And that's who she'll see."

Rand shrugged. "All right. Whatever you say. Let's go see her."

Gloria seized Rand's arm. "What about me?"

He jerked his arm away. "There's nothing more you can do here, Gloria. You've done enough for one day."

She crossed her arms, her voice whiny, defensive. "I was just trying to help, Rand. You needed to know the truth about that girl, and she obviously wasn't about to tell you."

Rand pushed his hair back from his forehead in a gesture of futility. "I don't want to talk about this now. Just go home, Gloria. Go home!"

With a withering glance at Becky, Gloria sneered. "A lot of thanks a girl gets for setting things straight. Next time do your own dirty work, Rand."

After Gloria had strutted off like a wounded peacock, Rand turned to Becky, his expression grim. "Ready to go in?"

Her nod was more an expression of bravado than confidence. She had no idea how Myrtle would respond to her. But no matter how she reacted, Becky had to see her and assure her of her love.

They walked in discomfiting silence down the long corridor to room 134. At the door Rand stopped and looked at Becky, his blue eyes clouded with reproach and pain. "No matter what our differences, when we enter this room, we're both cheerful and upbeat. Got it?"

"Of course." But in her heart of hearts, Becky wondered if she would ever feel happy again. Whatever joy she felt was withering, shrinking, shriveling into a cold, hard knot of misery and shame. *Heavenly Father, how did I make such a horrible mess of things? And how can I ever make things right?*

Please let me start by being a comfort to Myrtle. Don't let her suffer for what I've done.

They entered the darkened room, Becky first, then Rand, and quietly approached the bed where Myrtle lay slumbering. Tears sprang to Becky's eyes as she placed her hands on the cold metal side rails and gazed down at her friend. Myrtle looked so feeble, her translucent skin like crepe paper, her eyes ringed with deep shadows. Her thin body made only a small rise in the blankets.

Becky looked up at Rand. "Maybe we should just let her sleep."

"I suppose."

Myrtle stirred. "Rand?"

"Yes, Grams. I'm right here."

Her voice was faint. "I hurt."

Rand choked back a sob. "I know, Darling. You fell. But you're going to be fine."

"I'm so tired."

"The doctor gave you a sedative to help you sleep. You just need to rest."

Becky stroked Myrtle's gossamer hair. "I'm here too, Dear."

"Who is it?"

"Rebecca." She spoke in her natural voice.

"My friend?"

"Yes, it's me."

Myrtle held out a trembling hand. "Yes, I know you. My dear friend. I'm so glad you came."

"I wouldn't be anywhere else." Becky pressed the arthritic hand against her own warm cheek. "I love you, Myrtle."

Myrtle opened her clouded eyes and managed the hint of a smile. "You are. . .precious to me, Rebecca."

"As you are to me." Becky blinked back tears. "I'll be praying for you. Get well soon."

Rand spoke up, his voice uneven. "We're going now,

Grams. We want you to get some sleep, okay?"

"Come back soon, my darlings."

"We will." Becky kissed her forehead. "Sleep well."

Rand kissed his grandmother good-bye, then escorted Becky out of the room and down the hall to the lobby. Facing her, he assumed his lofty professorial air. "Thank you, Becky. You made my grandmother happy, and for that I'm grateful."

"I don't want your gratitude, Rand. I needed to be here for her."

He shifted his torso, looking ill at ease. "Do you want me to help you gather up your, uh, belongings in the waiting room?"

She had nearly forgotten the items Gloria had strewn about the place. "No, I'll get them. . .if someone hasn't already tossed them out."

"Fine. Then I'll let you be about your business."

She chewed her lower lip. *I can't let things end this way!* Gingerly she touched his arm. "We've got to talk, Rand. Please give me a chance to explain about Rebecca Sterling."

"I'm too exhausted to hash this out right now, Becky." He rubbed the back of his neck. "All I can think about is my grandmother and whether she's going to come through this okay."

"Later then?"

He shook his head, his eyes shadowed, grim. "I think we've said enough already. You played your little game and made a fool of me. Aren't you satisfied?"

"Satisfied?"

"Sure. I fell hook, line, and sinker for your charming little act—and for you." He made a derisive sound in his throat, low, guttural, not quite a laugh. "How bizarre is this anyway? You made me fall in love with an old lady who doesn't exist and a young woman who isn't the person I thought she was. Maybe that was part of your plan too."

"I didn't make you do anything, Rand!"

"Whatever your intentions, Becky, I wish I could say I

enjoyed your stellar performance." He pummeled his fist against his palm. "The funny thing is, I consider myself a smart, savvy guy. But you put me in my place. I didn't have a clue. If your goal was to make me feel like an idiot, you succeeded. What more is there to say?"

Scalding tears welled in Becky's eyes. "There's so much you don't understand, Rand."

He stared her down. "You've got that right. No matter what your excuse, I'll never understand."

She lifted her quivering chin, her teary eyes searching his. "Isn't there anything I can say to make this right?"

"What can you possibly say, Becky? Nothing can make this right."

Her tears spilled over her lids and streamed down her cheeks. "Then I guess there's nothing else to say. . .except good-bye."

He averted his gaze, blinking rapidly. "I think that's best. I'll make some excuse to Grams to explain Rebecca's absence."

"You don't want me seeing her again?"

"It would only make matters worse."

Becky's voice rose on a sob. "I hope you don't hate me, Rand."

"Hate you?" He stiffened his shoulders like a soldier warding off an enemy. "Don't you get it, Becky? I'm too numb to feel anything."

※

Bing Crosby was singing "White Christmas" on the radio while the tiny lights on Becky's artificial tree twinkled merrily. On the kitchen table, frosted sugar cookies glittered with red and green sprinkles and the sweet, steamy aroma of hot chocolate filled the air. Even Becky's friend, Lyn Orcutt, sipping her cocoa, had a sprig of mistletoe tucked in her carrot-red curls. Christmas cheer was everywhere these days, except in Becky's heart. On this chilly Saturday night, even Lyn, with her lilting laughter and saucy good humor, couldn't raise Becky's spirits.

And it wasn't for a lack of trying. Lyn had served up a

mishmash of lame jokes and comedic routines from her theater arts repertoire, but it had all fallen on deaf ears. Becky simply wasn't in the mood for levity.

"Hey, Girlfriend, how can I get a smile out of you? I've tried everything. Maybe I should stand on my head and recite the Gettysburg Address backward!"

"Save your strength, Lyn." Becky cupped her mug of hot chocolate, her palms savoring the warmth. "It'll take some time for me to get over the blahs."

"It can't happen soon enough for me." Lyn spooned a half-melted marshmallow from her cup and popped it into her mouth, leaving a white mustache on her upper lip. She raised her brows and rolled her eyes Groucho Marx-style.

Becky managed only a forced smile. "I appreciate your efforts, Lyn, but it'll take more than a few laughs to make me feel better."

"Okay, then let's get to the point. When you phoned, you said you had a favor to ask me. What is it?"

Becky stirred her hot chocolate for a long moment. "I was wondering. . .would you teach my Bible study class tomorrow night?"

"Teach your class? Sure. You won't be able to make it?"

"I'd just rather not go. I can't face a bunch of high school kids right now." Becky's voice wavered. "The truth is, how can I tell them they should be trusting and rejoicing in the Lord when I'm so miserable and pathetic right now. I refuse to be a hypocrite."

"You don't have to be, Beck."

"What? A hypocrite?"

"No. Pathetic and miserable."

"Lyn, if this is going to be a sermon. . ."

"Not at all. It's just that Jesus is always ready to help and comfort us, if we ask Him. It seems a shame to—"

"What? Wallow in my own misery?"

"Something like that."

"It's my misery, and I'll wallow in it if I want to." The illogical words struck them both funny. They broke into laughter, Becky chuckling in spite of herself.

Lyn reached for a sugar cookie, her third so far. "So, Beck, how long has it been since you've seen Professor Cameron?"

"Nearly a week."

"You haven't gone to class?"

"No. I've turned in my work, most of it anyway, but I can't bear to face him."

"What about finals next week?"

"Rand gave us a choice of writing a paper or taking a test. I wrote a paper and turned it in yesterday. It's not my best work, but it'll have to do."

"Then, even if you miss some classes, it shouldn't affect your grade?"

"I hope not. I'm sure Rand knows why I haven't been there. And he's probably relieved he hasn't had to face me either."

Lyn shook her head. "I'm so sorry your little masquerade broke up the two of you. If I'd had any idea where it would lead, I never would have suggested it in the first place."

"It's not your fault, Lyn. It was a great idea. Portraying an elderly woman was an experience I'll never forget. And I was able to get great material for my dissertation."

"I'm glad the experience wasn't all bad."

"The only bad part was that I didn't have enough faith in God and in Rand to tell him the truth from the beginning. I should have trusted more. I should have known God would work things out in His own way and that His way would be best. Instead, I let my fears and anxieties dictate what I did. I was foolish, but I can't change any of it now. I just have to go on from here."

"Was it worth it, Beck? Being Rebecca?"

Tears sprang to her eyes. "I'll tell you this, Lyn. I was a

better person as Rebecca Sterling than I ever was as Becky Chandler. God gave me a standard to live up to for the rest of my life." She grimaced. "But I guess so far I haven't done a very good job of living up to her example."

"You will, Beck. Wait and see."

"Meanwhile, I've got to finish writing my thesis and get through finals next week. Then you and I will be heading home to Seattle for the Christmas holidays."

Lyn clapped her hands together. "I can't wait. I'm already packed—well, almost."

"I can't think about packing until I turn in my thesis. On second thought, I'll take it with me and finish it at home. But at least I'm in the home stretch. Now just pray that my advisor thinks it's good."

"She will. And in January you'll be graduating with your doctorate degree. You'll be on top of the world, Girlfriend."

Becky sipped her hot chocolate. It was lukewarm now. "I'm not sure I'm even coming back for the ceremony."

Lyn stared at her. "Not come back? Why not? You've worked so hard for this. You've got to do the whole cap-and-gown bit."

"It's a mid-year graduation, Lyn. Small and low-key. Not like the big graduation ceremony in June with all the pomp and circumstance."

"What does that matter? It's still your graduation. You've got to be there."

Becky lowered her gaze, her index finger tracing a water ring on the table. "I can't risk running into Rand. I couldn't bear to see the disappointment and disapproval in his eyes."

"Don't you still love him?"

"Yes. With all my heart. That's why I can't face him again. It would break my heart. . .or what's left of my heart. The only way I can get over him is to make sure I never lay eyes on him again."

"And what about his grandmother? You love her too."

"Yes, I do. I've phoned the hospital every day to check on her, and she's doing well. They discharged her yesterday."

"She went back to Morning Glory?"

"No. She's not there. Definitely not there, thank God! I heard Rand took her home with him and hired a full-time caregiver."

"Aren't you going to phone Rand to find out for sure?"

"I can't. He doesn't want me to see his grandmother again, and I have to respect his wishes."

"So that's the end of it? You're putting that whole chapter of your life behind you?"

"I have just one loose end to tie up: the evidence proving the negligence and abuse at the nursing home."

"I thought you'd already turned it over to the police."

"I tried to. The day after I got the tape from Myrtle's room, I went to the police with a copy and told them my suspicions. They said if I wanted to leave the tape they'd look into it, but the officer said the images were dark enough that it would be hard to prove anything without Myrtle's testimony. The tape alone wasn't enough, so I decided I had to present a case with evidence so compelling they couldn't ignore it. To avoid turning in a hodgepodge of stuff they might discredit, I've been writing up everything I observed, with the dates and people involved."

"Good. You're building a case the police can't ignore."

"I hope so. Even if they don't find my statements credible, they just can't ignore what I've caught on tape."

"That diabolical attendant you've suspected for so long?"

"Right. Dirk Seuer. I know now why he chased me all over the nursing home trying to get my camcorder." Becky grimaced and added, "Too bad I didn't get that on tape."

Lyn sat forward, her eyes wide with curiosity. "What does it show?"

"Plenty. Myrtle's room was dark, but with the night-light and a ribbon of hall light, you can see Dirk slapping and shoving Myrtle when he was supposed to be helping her to the bathroom."

"He should be arrested!"

"I pray he will be when the police see my documentation supports what's on the tape. The only problem is a defense attorney will say it was too dark to positively identify Dirk Seuer as the man on the tape, and I'm not sure a jury would convict him without Myrtle's testimony. I don't know if Rand would put her through that."

"When will you turn it all in? This is pretty urgent business, Becky. Someone else could get hurt—if they haven't already."

"I know. That's why I'm trying to do this right and as quickly as possible. I don't want the police thinking I'm a hysterical troublemaker. But it would be even worse if Dirk found out the police are on to him and he disappeared before they could arrest him."

Lyn helped herself to another cookie. Between nibbles, she mused, "You've got an awful lot on your plate, Girlfriend. What happens if the police do nothing in spite of your evidence?"

Becky inhaled sharply, then let out a long sigh. "I don't know what I'd do. I'd have to find another way to stop Dirk Seuer. Just in case, I'm sending a copy of all the evidence to Rand and keeping a copy for myself."

"Good idea. But I'd get that stuff out of my hands as soon as possible. You don't want that maniac Dirk coming after you."

Becky shivered at the thought. "He wouldn't do that. He doesn't even know about me. He only knows the old Rebecca, and we both know she's gone."

Lyn placed her hand over Becky's, concern evident in her eyes. "Just the same, I'd watch my step, Girlfriend. You're playing with fire, and I'd sure hate to see you get burned."

fifteen

Becky placed the incriminating videotape and her detailed notations of nursing home abuse in a small box and sealed it with packing tape. Surely with this information the authorities would begin an investigation of Morning Glory and arrest the sinister attendant, Dirk Seuer.

She would deliver the package to the police department on her way out of town tomorrow after putting an identical package in the mail to Rand. Once he reviewed the shocking contents of the box, he would make sure the police took action.

"And that's all I can do to make things right." Gazing around her silent apartment, Becky shivered inside, and not just from the cold. With the setting of a pale, wintry sun, a chill had settled over the darkening room. Even her little Christmas tree looked bleak. A forlorn breeze sent dry leaves skittering outside her window. Of course, this was nothing like the frigid weather she would face in Seattle. But the iciness in her veins sprang from something else—the biting sting of loneliness and disappointment.

How she missed Rand! . . . And the fragile promise of a future together that had been snatched from her eager fingers. But the truth was, she couldn't blame anyone but herself. It was her own doing. Her own doubts and fears had cost her the man she loved. Why hadn't she been honest with Rand from the beginning?

She took a black marking pen and addressed the two packages—one to Rand, the other to the police. She'd already packed one set of the evidence for herself, just to be on the safe side.

144

Even if her hopes and dreams had fallen by the wayside, she could still accomplish something significant with this little package. It could save the lives of people she loved. "Lord Jesus, please protect the needy residents at the nursing home. Let this evidence be enough to keep them safe from harm." Her voice sounded jarringly loud in the empty room, reminding her how very alone she felt.

She missed Myrtle and the others. And as strange as it seemed, she missed her elderly alter ego, Rebecca Sterling, most of all. "Lord, when I was Rebecca Sterling, I wasn't shy and fearful and indecisive. Why can't I be that way as myself? Please let me have the courage, faith, and compassion Rebecca showed. When I walked in her shoes, I was a better person. I want to be like that again so I can honor and please You, Jesus." She heaved a sigh of discouragement. "But, Father, how can I please You when I've made such a mess of things and when I still feel so weak and fainthearted?"

Becky set the two packages on her rolltop desk, then glanced around. She would have to make sure to take her laptop and her latest copy of her dissertation. It was all but done. She would do her final rewrite at home in Seattle, then send it to her faculty advisor in time for her December 31 deadline. If the paper was acceptable, she would be graduating in January.

But she wasn't sure she would come back to Rockmount College to march in the ceremony. What if she saw Rand? She wasn't sure she could bear the humiliation. Perhaps she would just let Rockmount send her the diploma.

Are you running away again, Becky? Didn't you just say you wanted Rebecca's faith and courage? You won't find them by running.

"Lord, I'm not running! It's just. . . When I take my eyes off You, I get into trouble. Help me to give You my weaknesses so You can turn them into Your strengths."

She knew now that wearing the disguise in itself wasn't wrong; it was wrong for her to hide the truth from the people she loved out of fear they wouldn't understand or would misjudge her. More than anything, she wanted to surrender her hopes and expectations to Christ and leave her future in His hands.

She picked up yesterday's newspaper from the coffee table and was about to toss it into the waste basket when the doorbell rang. Who could it be? She gazed down at the old sweater and jeans she was wearing. She wasn't expecting any visitors at this time of evening. Not even Lyn, who was at her own apartment packing for their trip home tomorrow.

As Becky trudged to the door, she muttered under her breath, "If it's somebody selling magazines or wanting me to change my phone service, they're toast!"

"Who is it?" She gazed through the peephole, but the porch light was too dim for her to make out the person standing there holding. . .flowers? It couldn't be Rand, could it?

No answer, except for another knock.

Rolling up the newspaper, she called back, "If you're selling something, I don't want any!"

The knocking grew more insistent. Finally relenting, she opened the door a crack and peered out.

Dirk Seuer stared back at her.

Becky took an instinctive step backward, then gathered her wits and demanded, "What do you want?" *Stay calm, Beck. He doesn't know who you are.*

"I'm looking for Rebecca Sterling." In the shadows his towering frame took on ominous proportions. The small bouquet of flowers shuddered as he raised the collar of his overcoat against the chafing wind, and his narrow eyes glittered with an animal intensity. "She lives here, doesn't she?"

"Why do you want to know?" Becky held the door ajar just

enough for conversation, but she was ready to slam it shut if Dirk made a wrong move.

His eyes remained fixed on Becky. "I've got some news for her. Is she related to you?"

Becky felt a prickly sensation at the back of her neck. "What news?"

"Is she here or not?"

"I'm sorry. She's not available. You can tell me, and I'll pass on the information."

"Sorry. It's important. I need to see her personally." A corner of Dirk's lips twisted into a sneer. "If she's not here I could come in and wait."

Panic moved in Becky's chest. "That's not a good idea. Why don't you phone her tomorrow?"

"This can't wait, Miss. It's about her friend, Myrtle Watson."

"Myrtle? What about her?"

Dirk's rumbling voice fell to a whisper. "She died tonight."

"Died?" Becky's mind went blank except for a resounding Noooooo!

"I hate to be the bearer of such bad news. Mrs. Watson's nurse, Selena, sent me to inform her friend, Mrs. Sterling. I'd like to tell her myself. I know it'll be a shock. They were very close."

"Yes, they were." Becky allowed the door to swing open. She stepped back unsteadily, her thoughts reeling. She couldn't wrap her mind around such devastating news. "How did she die?"

Dirk stepped inside, handed her the bedraggled bouquet, then closed the door behind him and turned the lock. "She died in her sleep. Selena walked in and found her dead in her bed, looking peaceful as an angel."

An alarm sounded in Becky's head. The wilted flowers fell from her hands. "Selena found her? How could that be?"

Dirk took a step toward her, his strapping presence filling the room with a restive, malignant energy. "Selena was her nurse. She was on duty. What does it matter? The old woman is dead."

Something's wrong here. Help me, Lord Jesus! "Myrtle wasn't in the nursing home. Her grandson took her home with him."

"You got your facts wrong, Lady. Myrtle Watson died in her bed at Morning Glory."

Becky's voice wavered with emotion. "I don't believe you. I know for a fact Myrtle is staying with her grandson."

"Check again. He brought her back."

She moved toward the telephone. "I can call Rand easily enough and verify whether what you've said is true."

Dirk sprang forward and seized her wrist. "Don't do that."

When she struggled to pull her arm away, he tightened his grasp until she winced. "Hold your horses, Girlie!"

She spoke through clenched teeth. "Get out of here or I'll call the police."

"I'm not going anywhere until I talk to the old woman!"

"I told you, Rebecca Sterling isn't here."

"Then I'll wait. She has something I want, and I'm not leaving 'til I get it."

"What do you want?"

He tightened his grip. "She knows what it is."

"You can't talk to her."

"Says who?"

Becky's breath came in labored gasps. "She. . .she doesn't exist."

A diabolic gleam blazed in Dirk's eyes. "That's what I thought." He released her arm, then fished in his jacket pocket and produced a crumpled gray mass—Rebecca's wig! His surly voice boomed with triumph. "When I couldn't find the old woman that day, I finally decided to take another look in the public rest rooms. This time I took more than just a quick peek inside. I even rummaged through the trash. That's where I found the old lady disguise. Then I made the connection to you, the pretty girl walking out the door that day. You fooled us good with that old switcheroo. You're one brassy lady. Smart too. It took me awhile to track you down, but I finally did."

"How?"

"Since the old lady—you—walked to Morning Glory before you started driving over there, I figured you had to live nearby. I've been looking real hard for you and I finally saw you get out of your car yesterday. I just waited to see which apartment you went into. Now it's payback time for this scar you put on my forehead."

Becky shrank back. "I. . .I didn't mean to hurt you."

Dirk grinned, showing uneven teeth. "That's what I figured. So you just give me that videotape you took from Myrtle Watson's room and we'll call it even."

"I don't know what you're talking about." Slowly unrolling the newspaper in her hand, Becky inched toward her rolltop desk.

"Where is it? I'm not a patient man, Lady."

"I don't have your tape. If you don't believe me, check the video cabinet by the TV." As Dirk turned his gaze to the cabinet, Becky reached over to the desk and set the newspaper over her packages.

Dirk whirled back around, his dark eyes flashing. "Don't play games with me, Lady! Where's the tape? Give it to me or you'll be sorry."

Squaring her shoulders, Becky declared with more authority than she felt, "If you don't leave right this minute, I'll call the police."

Dirk crossed the room, gripped her arm, and twisted it behind her back. "I'm not leaving here without the tape. I'll turn this place upside down if I have to."

The phone rang, startling them both.

Dirk held her fast. "Don't answer it!"

"I've got to. It—it's my girlfriend. We're supposed to have

dinner together." Becky spoke over the pain coursing through her shoulder. "If I don't answer, she'll just come straight over to pick me up."

He released her. "Okay, pick it up. But if you say one wrong word, it'll be your last."

With trembling fingers Becky grabbed the receiver and said hello.

Tears sprang to her eyes when she heard Lyn's cheery, "Hi, Beck. You all packed?"

"No, Lyn." *Help me, Lord, to say the right words.* "I'm sorry, I'm not going to make it to dinner tonight."

"Dinner?" Lyn repeated. "We weren't doing dinner. We're packing, remember?"

"I'd love to join you at the coffeehouse, but I have a dinner date with Rand. It completely slipped my mind."

"A date with Rand? Your mind must have slipped a gear. Last I knew, you two weren't even speaking."

"That's right, Lyn." Becky's heart thumped against her rib cage like a tom-tom. "We're going to watch that Christmas video I've been wanting to show him for so long."

"Christmas video? Beck, what's going on? You're not making any sense."

Dirk gave Becky a menacing stare and hissed, "Hang up!"

Lord, help me! Give me Your strength before I faint dead away! "I've got to go, Lyn," she said breathlessly. "Rand should be here any moment."

"Girlfriend, are you okay?"

"No, not at all, Lyn. Thanks for calling."

"Wait, Beck. Something's wrong! Do you need help?"

"Absolutely! Let's get together soon, okay?"

Before she could hear Lyn's reply, Dirk grabbed the phone and disconnected it from the wall. "No more calls!" He shoved her toward the video cabinet. "Now find that tape, or you're dead meat!"

Becky stooped down beside the television set. "I'll play the tapes I have. You can check them all out. You'll see it's not here."

Dirk sat down on the sofa. "Hurry up. I ain't got all day."

She turned on the TV, put a cassette in the VCR, and pressed the remote control button. Familiar images flashed on the screen—Becky and her parents at last summer's family reunion in Seattle. A pang of regret spiked through her. *Dear Father in heaven, what if I never get to see my parents again? Please don't let this deranged man hurt me! Please get me out of this!*

"That's not it!" stormed Dirk. "Try another one!"

Over the next twenty minutes she played one tape after another. Some were personal videos, others were programs she had taped from the TV. She could tell by his seething countenance that Dirk was becoming more enraged by the moment.

"This is one of the last ones." She inserted another tape in the VCR. *Stall him for as long as you can, Becky, and pray that someone comes to your rescue!* The tape flickered for a moment, then wonderful images of Christmas two years ago filled the screen. Her mother was laughing as her father opened his gift—a garish red tie with reindeer and mistletoe on it. Becky remembered the moment, especially her father's amused expression. She was laughing so hard she couldn't hold the camera still. Soon everyone was laughing.

Dirk jumped up from the sofa and snatched the remote control from her hand. "What are you trying to pull, showing lame stuff like this? Where's the tape you made in Myrtle Watson's room?"

Becky's throat tightened. "I told you I don't have it."

Dirk wrapped his thick fingers around her neck until she gasped for air. "That's not good enough, Missy. Get me that tape. Now!"

As he released her, she collapsed on the floor. Her throat ached; she couldn't swallow. Rubbing her bruised neck, she tried to speak, but no words came. She stumbled to her feet, but Dirk was right behind her. His hefty arm snaked around her neck in a painful hammerlock. As his massive frame imprisoned her, she felt his hot, garlic-tainted breath against her ear. "If you wanna come out of this alive, little girl, get me that tape!"

The doorbell rang and a familiar masculine voice called out, "Becky! Let me in!"

Rand's voice!

Dirk tightened his hold. "What's he doing here?"

Becky struggled to speak, but all she could utter was a single word: "Date."

Dirk uttered something unintelligible under his breath.

"Becky!" Rand was pounding on the door now. "Open up!"

Dirk seized her by the hair, yanking her head back. "Tell him to go away. You don't want to see him."

Tears flooded Becky's eyes. "He won't believe me."

"Tell him anyway!"

"Go away, Rand!" she rasped. "Leave me alone!"

"Let me in, Becky!"

"I can't! Go away, Rand!"

She heard an enormous thump against the door, then another. The walls shook and the windows rattled. Before she could comprehend what was happening, the door burst open and Rand came bounding in. Dirk released Becky and raised his arms in self-defense as Rand tackled him. The two men struggled for several moments, knocking over knick-knacks and nearly toppling the artificial Christmas tree.

Becky stepped back and watched in bewilderment, her mind reeling with disbelief. *This can't be happening!*

Dirk picked up a silver candlestick and swung it at Rand's head just as Rand delivered a knockout punch to Dirk's jaw. The burly man staggered, then slowly crumpled to the floor. Rand stared down at him, then nudged him with his shoe to make sure he was unconscious. Breathing hard, Rand raked his tousled hair back from his forehead, then turned to Becky and opened his arms wide. Terrified, she ran to him for an embrace. His sturdy arms enveloped her as he nuzzled her hair with his chin.

"Becky, are you okay?"

"I think so. Thank God you came."

"Thank your friend Lyn too. She phoned me."

He held her close and rubbed her neck as sirens sounded in the distance. After several moments, she heard a commotion outside and looked around to see Lyn and two police officers entering her apartment.

Lyn ran to Becky and hugged her. "Beck, I was so scared. I didn't know if we'd get here in time."

"Oh, thank you, Lyn. I wasn't sure whether you'd realize I was in trouble or just think I was talking crazy."

"You said you had a date with Rand to watch a video. I knew that was impossible, so you had to be sending me a secret message. I called Rand to make sure you didn't have a date. When I told him about the evidence you'd gathered against Dirk, he told me to call the police."

The two officers yanked Dirk Seuer to his feet and handcuffed him. One turned to Becky as they pushed their prisoner toward the door. "Miss Chandler, we'd like you to come by the station tonight and make a statement so we can press charges against this man."

"I'd be glad to. I have some evidence for you as well." She retrieved one of the boxes from her desk and handed it to the officer. "Everything you need to know, including why he came after me, should be in here."

"Thanks, Miss Chandler. Believe me, we'll handle this with care."

Lyn gave Becky a quick hug. "I'm going home, but if you need anything, call me, and I'll be over in a flash."

"Thanks, Lyn. I don't know what I would have done without you."

"No problem, Girlfriend. You gave good clues. It didn't take me long to connect the dots." Lyn rolled her eyes toward Rand. "Now you two get things straightened out here, okay?"

Becky smiled. "I'll do my best."

After everyone had left, Rand drew her into his arms again. "Girl, you scared me out of my wits. Why didn't you tell me about your undercover detective work? This was much too dangerous a situation for you to handle alone."

"I was going to tell you as soon as I gathered enough evidence to convict Dirk Seuer."

"You could have been killed."

"God took care of me."

Rand held her close. "When I think of what might have happened if we hadn't arrived when we did. . .I couldn't have forgiven myself if that beast had hurt you. Thank God I live only a few minutes away and was home when Lyn called."

"I was so afraid she wouldn't get what I was trying to say."

"You never should have done this by yourself, Becky. Why didn't you tell me what you were doing?"

"Well, lately we haven't exactly been talking."

Rand turned her face up to his. She winced at the unexpected hurt in his eyes. "You should have trusted me enough to tell me, Becky. I could have helped you. I could have made sure you didn't endanger your life. Why didn't you trust me enough to tell me the truth?"

She pulled away from him. "I don't know, Rand. I figured I could handle things by myself. You were so angry with me for disguising myself as Rebecca Sterling."

"I'm not angry anymore, Becky. Disappointed, perplexed, yes. You didn't trust me enough to confide in me about your little subterfuge. But I overreacted. Since that day in the hospital, I've been putting some pieces together and gaining some perspective. I know you weren't trying to hurt me. And your advisor let me know your disguise was part of your research project for your dissertation. But why you didn't tell me that, I'll never know. "

"I tried to, Rand, a hundred different times."

"Yes, I suppose you did. And there were times when I wasn't ready to listen. So I'm at fault too."

"Does this mean you forgive me?"

"Forgiveness isn't the issue, Becky. I do forgive you. I hold no ill will against you. But that doesn't change anything between us." His voice drifted off, as if he were mulling over a familiar theme. "I've thought about this over and over, and I can come to only one conclusion. Obviously our relationship hasn't reached the level of mutual candor and transparency I had hoped for. Trust is the cornerstone of a relationship, and we don't have that."

Becky lowered her lashes and bit her lower lip. "I'm sorry, Rand. All I can say is, I never intended to deceive you."

"I know you didn't. That's the irony of it all. It just keeps happening anyway, doesn't it? And there doesn't seem to be a thing either of us can do about it." He scratched his head. "Listen, do you want me to drive you to the police station?"

"No, I can do it. I've bothered you enough for one night. Besides, I may be there awhile, and I'm sure you have class in the morning." *What am I saying? Of course I want you to go with me! But I'm too proud or stupid to admit it! Please insist on going with me anyway!*

Rand glanced at his watch. "All right, if you're sure. Then I suppose I should be going."

Disappointment sliced through her. A crisis had brought them together tonight for a few remarkable moments. Now he was walking out of her life again—and she was letting him go!

She reached for the remaining package on her desk. "I was going to mail this to you, Rand, but you might as well take it now."

He accepted the box with a quizzical glance. "What is it?"

"It's a copy of the videotape that proves Dirk Seuer manhandled your grandmother, along with other evidence of abuse and negligence I documented at Morning Glory."

Rand turned the package over in his hands, then tucked it in his overcoat pocket. "Your friend Lyn mentioned one of the reasons for your disguise was to gather evidence of abuse at the nursing home. Whatever you found brought Dirk Seuer gunning for you. But I have no idea what the whole story is."

"You'll find out when you look over the material in the box."

His fingertips grazed her arm. "Are you going to be available, in case I have any questions?"

"I don't think so." She picked at a frayed spot on her shabby sweater. She was wearing her grubbiest clothes, her hair was flying in every direction at once from her scuffle with Dirk Seuer, and she didn't have on a speck of makeup! She couldn't possibly look worse. *Story of my life. Always leading with the wrong foot, saying the wrong thing, making a fool of myself. . .*

"Why not?"

"I leave in the morning for Seattle. Lyn and I are going home for the holidays."

"You'll be back, won't you? After all, you graduate in January."

Hugging herself, she rocked on her heels, scouring her mind for the right words. "I'm not sure I'm coming back, Rand."

"What do you mean? You have to come back."

"Not really." Even to herself, her voice sounded heavy, wooden, the words coming out rote, canned, lacking conviction. "I can receive my diploma without marching in the graduation ceremonies."

"But why would you want to miss such an important occasion?"

"I have to look for a job in Seattle." She was digging herself in deeper, but she couldn't seem to stop herself. "There are some wonderful hospitals there. I'm hoping to land a position as a geriatric therapist."

Rand's mouth sagged. "So you plan to make Seattle your home?"

"It is my home. My parents are there. It's where I grew up. I see no reason not to go back." *Unless you give me a reason, Rand. Please tell me you want me to stay here. Please tell me we still have a chance for a life together!*

Rand massaged his knuckles as if his hands were cold. "Those are compelling reasons for going home to Seattle." His gaze met hers. "I hope you'll be happy there, Becky. You deserve to be happy. You've meant a great deal to me and my grandmother."

Tears welled in her eyes. "How is she. . .your grandmother? You haven't told me."

"She's fine." Rand cracked his knuckles several times. "When she was released from the hospital, I took her home to my place. I've hired a live-in caregiver, and it's working well so far. Thank God I got her away from Morning Glory!"

"Yes, thank God. I had heard Myrtle was living with you now, and I was so relieved."

"You could come by and see her if you have time—before you leave, I mean."

"I'm afraid Lyn and I need to get an early start in the morning. It's a long drive to Seattle."

"Sure. I understand. I'll give my grandmother your regards."

"Yes, please do. I love her very much." *And I love you too, Rand! Don't you see it? Don't you know? Do I have to shout it to the heavens?*

"I know you love her. And she loves you too."

What about you, Rand? Don't you love me enough to forgive

me for my deceptions and insist I stay here with you? Why are you letting me walk out of your life forever?

They walked in silence to the door. Gripping the knob, Rand turned to face her. In the rosy lamplight of her apartment, he looked like a tall and handsome Sir Lancelot, her gallant hero. Instinctively she reached up and touched his bronzed cheek. "Thanks for rescuing me tonight, Rand. I'll never forget it."

"Nor will I. I'm a little rusty when it comes to rescuing damsels in distress. I'm just thankful God gave us His hand of protection."

"Yes, He's always there for us. But sometimes I forget."

"So do I. But He's faithful even when we're not."

"Yes, He is. Praise Him for that." She wanted to say more, to spill out all the churning, conflicting emotions surging in her heart of hearts. But the words died on her lips. As an uneasy silence lengthened between them, Rand opened the door. A chill breeze swept over her, making her shiver.

Rand looked down at her, the sharp angles of his face twisted in a grimace of pain. "I guess this is good-bye, Becky."

She bit her lip. "Yes, I suppose it is. One more good-bye." She still cradled her arms against her chest. She had the sensation if she didn't hold on tight, her heart would shatter in a million pieces. In spite of her best efforts to control her emotions, a recalcitrant tear spilled onto her cheek. Her face heating with embarrassment, she wiped the wetness away with a vigorous sweep of her hand. Blinking rapidly, she forced a bright, brittle smile in place. "I wish you the best, Rand. Good night."

"Same here." He hesitated. "May I kiss you good-bye? For old time's sake?" Before she could reply, he brushed a sweet, warm kiss across her lips that left her dazzled, blindsided. Then, without another word, he strode out the door and down the sidewalk and disappeared into the night.

Dazed and trembling, Becky shut the door, turned the lock, then pressed her back against the door. For a long moment she held her breath, praying that Rand would return, knock on her door, and tell her he couldn't leave until she knew how much he loved her. She waited until she heard the rumble of his automobile as he pulled away from her apartment.

Then all was silent. Except for the sounds gathering deep in her chest, rising up and bursting through her dry lips in a racking, excruciating wail. Slowly she slid down the length of the door until she was sitting on the floor, a hapless, sobbing, inconsolable child in a grubby sweater and jeans, a stubborn, silly, fretful girl who could not let herself be comforted even by the still, small voice of God.

sixteen

"Lyn, I'm not going to graduate after all!" Gripping the telephone receiver to her ear, Becky could hardly keep the hysteria out of her voice. "I know he's doing it just to spite me, Lyn. Can you believe it? I'm so angry I could spit nails. Here it is only the second day of January, and he's already spoiled my new year!"

Lyn, on the other end of the line, came back with a baffled, "Slow down, Beck. Who's spoiled your new year? And why won't you graduate? Wasn't your dissertation approved?"

"Yes, it was approved. Several days ago. That's not the problem."

"Then what?"

"You won't believe this, Lyn. That man is spiteful and ruthless and—"

"What man?"

"Rand Cameron! Lyn, he's giving me an incomplete in his class!"

"You've got to be kidding!"

"I'm dead serious. My mom just brought in the mail. I got a notice from the school. He claims I didn't turn in a required paper. Can you believe Rand would do this to me? If I weren't here in Seattle, I'd march into his office and give him a piece of my mind."

"Listen, Beck, maybe it's not too late to turn in the paper. Have you tried calling him?"

"Yes, but he's off campus for Christmas break, and when I phoned his house all I got was his answering machine."

"What are you going to do, Beck? You've got to graduate."

"I'm thinking of going back to school early so I can straighten out this mess. Would you mind going back early?"

"No problem, Girlfriend. I think my folks are ready for me to head back to school and give them a little peace and quiet anyway. When do you want to go?"

"Is tomorrow too soon?"

"Tomorrow? I'll have some major packing to do, what with all my Christmas loot, but I think I can be ready."

"Terrific. I'll pick you up after breakfast. Let's just pray the weather cooperates and gives us sunny skies."

❧

A torrential rain greeted them as they headed south out of Seattle the next morning. Even with her windshield wipers swishing at full force, Becky could hardly see the road ahead. The whole miserable landscape seemed washed with huge, gray, streaming tears. Like the angry, aching, unshed tears inside her.

Lyn turned up the heat. "Can't wait to be back in sunny California."

"I can." Becky spoke over the droning rain. "I wouldn't be going back to Rockmount if I didn't have to."

"I know. You didn't want to see Professor Cameron again, did you?"

"Not in a million years." Becky glanced over at her friend, then back at the gloomy road. At least the downpour was letting up a little. "I thought I had everything worked out so well, Lyn. I had accepted the idea that I would stay in Seattle. I've already submitted applications for a geriatric therapist position to several Washington hospitals. I thought I was getting over Rand. I hoped I could put this whole semester behind me and concentrate on the future. Then Rand does something so cruel and unexpected, my feelings are all messed up again."

Lyn adjusted the heat. "Too hot in here now!"

"If you're talking about my temper—"

"No way. I don't blame you for hating the guy, Beck. He fixed it so you can't graduate."

"I do hate him, and I love him, and I'm furious with him, and I want him more than ever!"

"You do have it bad."

"Do you think he's trying to spite me for deceiving him with my Rebecca Sterling disguise? Guys hate being made a fool of."

"I never thought of Professor Cameron as a vindictive man, but something's obviously going on here."

As the rain subsided to a fine gray mist, Becky accelerated her vehicle. As much as she dreaded returning to California and confronting Rand Cameron, she didn't want to spend forever slogging over clogged, rain-slick roads.

"Hey, Girlfriend, are you in a hurry or what?"

Becky heaved a disgruntled sigh. "I just want to get this whole thing with Rand over with and get on with my life."

"Hey, Beck, I've been thinking. Maybe this isn't one of nature's pesky interruptions. It could be God's divine appointment."

"Now you're sounding like Myrtle Watson."

"Is that so bad?"

Becky managed a smile. "No, it's a good thing, Lyn. In fact, since I've been home, I've spent a lot of time thinking and praying about my relationship with God. And, you know, I really want to be more like Myrtle Watson."

"Yeah? How so?"

"I don't know how to describe it, but she has this way of communing with God that's amazing. She makes it look so easy, so natural and ordinary. She just carries on this running conversation with Him all the time. She sees everything that happens to her through the filter of God's love. Nothing shakes her faith because she keeps her eyes on Jesus. Even with all the trauma she experienced at Morning Glory, her faith never wavered."

"Maybe that comes with being eighty years old and having lived through so much. A person just gets wiser with age."

"It's more than that, Lyn. Myrtle has an emotional connection with Jesus that keeps her on track, no matter what. I want that for my own life. I want to keep my eyes and heart fixed on Him. And I thought I was doing so well, until I got that notice I couldn't graduate because of the incomplete grade Rand gave me. Now, when I should be fixing my eyes on Jesus, all I can see is red."

Lyn turned up the heat again. "Then let your anger be the trigger that turns your eyes back to Jesus."

The windows were fogging up, so Becky turned on the defroster. "How so?"

"Look at it this way. Our negative feelings can be our temperature gauge. When the bad stuff starts raining down on us, we know it's time to scoot back under the umbrella of Christ's love."

"Speaking of umbrellas, did you bring one?"

"It's in my suitcase."

"A lot of good it will do there."

"We won't need it when we get to sunny California."

"You hope!"

They were silent for awhile, listening to the steady swish of windshield wipers and the swooshing, grating din of tires on wet pavement.

After awhile, Lyn said, "So is it true you didn't complete all your work for Professor Cameron's class? Or is he just trying to give you a hard time?"

Becky didn't answer right away. Finally she conceded, "I honestly don't know. I did skip the last few classes. After that terrible incident in the hospital, when Gloria came parading in with my wigs and those thrift shop clothes, and humiliated me in front of Rand, I just couldn't go back to class. I figured he would understand and not hold it against me for missing a few assignments."

"Evidently a wrong assumption."

"Definitely. He's out for retribution and not about to show mercy."

"When are you going to see him?"

"Tomorrow morning, if possible."

"Classes won't be in session for a couple more weeks."

"I know. I'll go to the faculty offices. He'll probably be there recording semester grades."

Lyn reached over and squeezed Becky's shoulder. "I'll be praying for you, Girlfriend. Praying real hard."

"Thanks. I need every prayer I can get."

&

The next morning, as Becky marched down the hall toward Rand's office, she thought about Lyn and her prayers. *I hope you're praying right this minute, Lyn, because right now I feel like I don't have a prayer. I'm walking to my own doom. The last thing I want to do is face Rand again and stir up all those buried feelings. I don't want him to see how vulnerable and weak I feel. My whole life is in his hands, and I hate it. After all that's happened, I hate having to ask him for anything.*

Just outside of Rand's office, Becky paused and closed her eyes. Her heart was pounding so fiercely she could hardly string together two coherent thoughts. *Please, Jesus, help me. I know I don't turn to You often enough. I try to do things on my own, and I'm always messing up. But what I really want is to please You. I give up my rights to myself. Do what You will today, and I thank You for it, because I know You love me and want what's best for me.*

When she opened her eyes, Rand Cameron filled her line of vision. He had opened the door and stood staring down at her, his brow furrowed.

With an unceremonious step backward, she blurted, "What are you doing here?"

"It's my office. What are you doing here?"

This wasn't the way she had planned things. Already she was tongue-tied and starting off on the wrong foot—literally! "I. . .I came to see you about my grade. My incomplete. Because of you, I can't graduate."

In his most professorial tone, he said, "Come inside. We'll talk about it."

As she followed him into his office and sat down in the straight-backed chair he offered her, she wondered if she would burst into tears. She felt like a schoolgirl being sent to the principal's office for some silly misdeed, like throwing spit wads at her neighbor or coloring the sidewalk with chalk. She squared her shoulders and lifted her chin defiantly. *I won't cry! I won't! I won't!*

Rand sat down behind his desk. "I'm sorry, Becky, but you didn't finish your class work. I had no choice but to turn in an incomplete."

She thought of a dozen arguments she wanted to fling at him, but she couldn't utter a single word.

Rand sat forward and tented his fingers. "You could make up the work and still graduate."

"I can?"

"Yes, I'll give you the assignments, and when you've completed them, I'll put in a grade change with the records office. You should still be able to march with your class."

She nodded. "That's all I wanted. Thank you."

The creases in his brow deepened. "Don't thank me. I'd do this for any student who's willing to do her work."

"I know. I wasn't suggesting you were playing favorites."

He raised one brow. "But you are, you know."

"What?"

"My favorite." He said the word so softly, she almost

missed it. Before she could analyze its implications, he stood up and said in his briskly professional voice, "So if there's nothing more. . ."

She stood up too. "I suppose not. Thank you for making this so easy."

Sadness edged his voice. "There's nothing easy about it, Becky."

"I suppose not." She took a step toward the door, then turned to face him. "Before I go, how is your grandmother?"

"She's doing well. She misses you."

Becky's voice caught. "I miss her too."

Rand came around the desk and approached her, his eyes as intensely blue as the ocean depths. "I want to thank you again for all you did to save her from the abuse she suffered at the hands of Dirk Seuer. I went over all the materials you gave me, including the videotape, and I'm amazed at your diligence and thoroughness." His voice took on an unexpected tenderness. "I understand now why you did what you did, wearing the disguise and all. You were a very brave lady. My grandmother and I owe you a debt of gratitude."

"I–I'm glad I was able to help."

"Seuer's been indicted, you know."

"No, I didn't know."

"And the authorities have begun an investigation of the nursing home. There are still a few bad apples mingling with the caring, qualified staff members. It'll be a better place when they're weeded out."

Becky massaged her knuckles. Her hands had never felt so clammy and cold. "Then it looks like everything has turned out well."

He nodded. "Almost everything."

There seemed to be nothing more to say, so she reached for the doorknob. *Lord Jesus, is this the way You want it to end? With just a sigh and a whimper?*

"Wait. Your assignments." Rand snatched up a folder from his desk and handed it to her.

"You had them all ready for me?"

"I figured you'd come see me. You wouldn't let one incomplete keep you from graduating."

"So you were expecting me."

"Let's say I was hoping you'd come."

She turned the folder over in her hands. She flipped through the pages. Rand had obviously taken a great deal of care in preparing her assignments. He wasn't just being inflexible and vindictive after all. "I'll get these back to you as soon as possible."

"I know you will."

She opened the door a crack. *Lord, what do You want me to do? Just leave? Forget everything Rand and I shared, the love blossoming between us? Help me, Father, to do what pleases You!* She thought of the verse, *Speaking the truth in love.* God willing, that's what she would do. She turned back to Rand and inhaled sharply.

"Was there something else, Becky?"

"Yes." *Help me, Lord! Give me the right words!* "I just want to say, Rand—"

He drew closer, his eyes filled with a vivid intensity. "Yes?"

Her voice wavered. "The last time we talked, you said trust is the cornerstone of a relationship. You said we didn't have it, and that's why we can't be together."

"I'm not sure those were my exact words. . ."

"Close enough." The fresh lime scent of his aftershave sent her mind pinwheeling. She closed her eyes and let the words tumble out pell-mell. "Before we just throw away our relationship, Rand, there are some things you need to know about me. I'm an only child. Growing up, I was a quiet, solitary girl."

"I know that."

"I'm also independent and stubborn and very shy. I have a

hard time talking to people, and it's not easy for me to confide my feelings."

"I know that too."

"But when I became Rebecca Sterling, I discovered a side to myself I never knew existed. God used Rebecca to teach me so many things about myself. He used her to make me a better person and to give me a high standard to strive for. He gave me the courage to speak out and fight for what's right and protect people who are weak and helpless."

"That's all very admirable, Becky."

"But I'm not perfect, Rand. I was wrong not to tell you the truth, but it was never because I wanted to deceive you or make a fool of you. That's the last thing I'd ever want to do, because I respect and admire you more than any man I've ever known."

Rand nodded, his expression solemn. "I believe you, Becky."

She rushed on, her words spilling out in surging heart swells of emotion. "I was just caught up in something I didn't know how to handle, Rand. And the truth is, I do trust you. I trusted you enough to fall in love with you. And I want you to know you can trust me, because every day I'm learning to trust God more, and He's making me the kind of woman you need. And if you can't see that, you're just blind and you're going to miss out on something wonderful. And that would be a real shame, Rand, because what we have is so rare and special. And I don't want to let it go."

Her lower lip trembled, making her words bobble unevenly. "So that's it, Rand. I just. . .I just wanted you to know I love you with all my heart. I. . .I think you love me, too. And I think God takes pleasure in seeing us together. That's the best reason of all to give our relationship another chance." She clasped her hands to her lips briefly. "And I can't believe I'm saying all this to your face. I'm either crazy in love or just plain crazy!"

As she paused to catch her breath, she noticed Rand was smiling. "Are you laughing at me? I knew I should have kept my mouth shut. Now that I've totally humiliated myself, I'm leaving! I'm just going to slink away somewhere, curl up, and die."

"Slow down, Sweetheart." Rand reached out and pulled her into his arms. "You aren't going anywhere, my darling. Not after that beautiful confession. You poured out your heart, knowing I could have trampled it. In my book, that's trust. Simple, beautiful honesty and trust." He bent his head toward hers and kissed her soundly, stealing her breath away.

When her lips were free again, she murmured, "Rand, are you saying. . . ?"

With his fingertip he traced the outline of her mouth. "I'm saying every word you said is true, Becky. I love you and I know you love me. And love like that deserves a leap of faith. It took me awhile to realize it, and by the time I did, you had run home to Seattle. I had to get you back here to see if what we have is real. And now, this moment, I know it is."

"That's why you gave me that incomplete? To get me back here?"

"That and the fact that you hadn't done all your work. I wouldn't have been a very good teacher if I'd let you get by with it, would I?"

"I suppose not."

"And now we have some homework to do together."

"More homework?"

He pulled her against his chest. "I think you'll like this homework, Sweetheart. It involves a lot of talking and kissing and sharing our hearts, plus a whole lot of praying to see what God has for us as a couple. If I'm reading Him right, there are some important events in our future."

"Our future? I like the sound of that." She felt suddenly euphoric, daring, flirtatious. "Tell me, Darling!"

"First, a graduation. I'm going to be there in the front row watching you receive your diploma."

"I can't wait, Rand. And then?"

"And then a wedding. And what a wedding it will be! A chapel full of flowers and a bride and groom surrounded by everyone they love. But they'll have eyes only for each other."

She laughed lightly, her spirits soaring. "I love it! I think we're reading the same book."

He matched her laughter. "You mean we're finally on the same page? Amazing!"

"The same page, the same paragraph, the same words. I love you, Rand, with all my heart."

"Yes, Darling, those are the very words I had in mind."

With exquisite tenderness he moved his lips over hers and whispered the promise she had waited a lifetime to hear. "I love you with all my heart, Becky. Marry me. I'll never let you go!"

A Letter To Our Readers

Dear Reader:

In order that we might better contribute to your reading enjoyment, we would appreciate your taking a few minutes to respond to the following questions. We welcome your comments and read each form and letter we receive. When completed, please return to the following:

Fiction Editor
Heartsong Presents
PO Box 719
Uhrichsville, Ohio 44683

1. Did you enjoy reading *Beguiling Masquerade* by Carole Gift Page?
   ❏ Very much! I would like to see more books by this author!
   ❏ Moderately. I would have enjoyed it more if

   _____

   _____

   _____

2. Are you a member of **Heartsong Presents**? ❏ Yes ❏ No
   If no, where did you purchase this book? _____

   _____

3. How would you rate, on a scale from 1 (poor) to 5 (superior), the cover design? _____

4. On a scale from 1 (poor) to 10 (superior), please rate the following elements.

   _____ Heroine   _____ Plot
   _____ Hero   _____ Inspirational theme
   _____ Setting   _____ Secondary characters

5. These characters were special because?_____

_____

_____

6. How has this book inspired your life?_____

_____

_____

7. What settings would you like to see covered in future
   Heartsong Presents books? _____

_____

_____

8. What are some inspirational themes you would like to see
   treated in future books? _____

_____

_____

9. Would you be interested in reading other **Heartsong
   Presents** titles? ❑ Yes ❑ No

10. Please check your age range:
    ❑ Under 18   ❑ 18-24
    ❑ 25-34   ❑ 35-45
    ❑ 46-55   ❑ Over 55

Name_____

Occupation _____

Address _____

City_____ State_____ Zip_____

Novel Crimes

4 stories in 1

*W*hen four women begin writing mysteries, they suddenly find themselves entering new lives of intrigue, danger—even love. Will their longing for adventure on paper take them to perilous places in real life?

In this intriguing novella compilation, you'll meet four fascinating women:

While these women plot intrigue, could God be plotting a much larger story—one involving love?

Contemporary, paperback, 352 pages, 5 $\frac{3}{16}$"x 8"

❤ • ❤ • ❤ • ❤ • ❤ • ❤ ❤ ❤ • ❤ • ❤ • ❤ • ❤ • ❤

❤ • ❤ • ❤ • ❤ • ❤ • ❤ ❤ ❤ • ❤ • ❤ • ❤ • ❤ • ❤

Heartsong

CONTEMPORARY ROMANCE IS CHEAPER BY THE DOZEN!

Any 12 Heartsong Presents titles for only $30.00*

Buy any assortment of twelve *Heartsong Presents* titles and save 25% off of the already discounted price of $3.25 each!

*plus $2.00 shipping and handling per order and sales tax where applicable.

HEARTSONG PRESENTS TITLES AVAILABLE NOW:

(If ordering from this page, please remember to include it with the order form.)

----- **Presents** -----

Great Inspirational Romance at a Great Price!

Heartsong Presents books are inspirational romances in contemporary and historical settings, designed to give you an enjoyable, spirit-lifting reading experience. You can choose wonderfully written titles from some of today's best authors like Hannah Alexander, Andrea Boeshaar, Yvonne Lehman, Tracie Peterson, and many others.

When ordering quantities less than twelve, above titles are $3.25 each.
Not all titles may be available at time of order.